WITH THIS SECRET

A SECOND CHANCE ROMANCE

GEORGIA LE CARRE

With This Secret

ISBN: 978-1-910575-32-1

Many, many thanks to:
Leanore Elliott
Caryl Milton
Nichola Rhead
Kirstine Moran
Brittany Urbaniak
Teresa Banschbach
Tracy Gray

PROLOGUE

BIANCA

(College Days)

https://www.youtube.com/watch?v=raNGeq3_DtM

Help, I am about to do something insane, I wrote to my best friend, Aldie.

While I waited for her response to come into our chat room, my gaze fluttered above to reread what I'd just typed. I tapped my fingers impatiently on the desktop and wondered why I was waiting for her response when I didn't really want her to talk me out of my intention.

Ten seconds later, I'd had enough.

Exiting the chat room, I pulled up his contact on my phone. The crazy message I'd just painstakingly crafted was there, still waiting for me to do something with it. Send or delete.

I glanced at the computer screen. Still no reply from her.

I took a deep breath and let my finger hover over the send button, but to my surprise, I couldn't let my message fly off into the ether. It was the sound of a message from Aldie pinging its way into my computer that jolted me into action. She was going to ask me to delete the message. I knew then what I wanted to do. I said a silent desperate prayer, let my finger drop on the send button, then went after Aldie's message.

She had a one word answer for me. *What?*

My fingers got busy. *You're too late. I've just told Levan that I'm in love with him.*

Her reply was as instantaneous. *You really used the word love?*

I could feel my heart start sinking. *Is that really bad?*

The seconds ticked by without response, even though I could see my message had been read.

I hate you, I wrote.

She came back with a hysterically laughing emoji and a message. *What did he say back?*

I swallowed hard. *He hasn't responded yet.*

I could picture her sighing. *Paste what you wrote here.*

I did as she asked and a couple of minutes passed with no reply from her. I wanted to strangle her.

ALDIE! I punched in.

She responded with a giggling emoji. *Well, I guess, you were honest and a tad bit eager, but ... at least you're breaking out of your damn shell.*

When Aldie used words like a tad bit, it was never a good thing. My nerves began to buzz with the very devastating possibility that I might have just sounded too desperate and blown up everything with Levan.

Do you think I should have waited? I asked anxiously. *I know he is, you know, out of my league. He's obviously from a very wealthy family. All those bodyguards hanging around outside the college gates. Not to mention we're still not certain of who he is exactly.*

Her reply was immediate. *He's not out of your league, babe. Yeah sure, he's gorgeous as fuck and obviously wealthy, but you're good enough for anyone, even him. Let's just wait and see what he replies back, okay?*

I closed my eyes for a second. *Okay, let's wait and see, and I know you think it's too soon and we haven't even had sex yet, but when you know, you know. And I've really fallen hard for him. Besides, I don't want to play games. I hate that.*

It took a bit longer for Aldie's answer. *It's never a good idea to wear your heart on your sleeve or anywhere it can be easily trampled on. Men are class A bastards when they know you're crazy about them. So just cool it, okay.*

I didn't tell her I thought I was already more than half way in love with Levan. Sadly, I wrote my reply to her. *Okay. I will cool the ardor.*

That's my girl, she came back. *I just got out of class, I'm hurrying to an open house in East Village, but I'll stop by your bakery when I'm done.*

Nah, my mom is working there today. I'm in the library, then I'm going home, I responded. I paused a moment then added hopefully, *I'll text you when he replies.*

Cool. Can't wait to hear what he says.

I waited and I waited, but Levan never called or wrote back. He literally disappeared into thin air. It hurt like mad, but I took full responsibility for the disaster. I had pathetically worn my heart on my sleeve, and he, being the bastard he was, had stomped all over it. I would never see his laughing gray eyes again. But that was okay. I was strong. I would harden my heart and get over him if it was the last thing I did.

1

LEVAN

Present Day
https://www.youtube.com/watch?v=nKhNıt_7PEY

I was sitting at the bar of a French seafood restaurant in Midtown Manhattan, and had just taken a sip of wine, when she emerged from the restroom area.

Doubling over in shock, I nearly choked on my wine.

My unguarded reaction immediately raised the alarm of the two men with me. They shot their gazes around instantly, searching for any signs of danger.

"Is there a problem?" Sergei asked in low urgent tones, his hand going to his concealed weapon.

"No, no," I said quickly, raising a reassuring hand. "There's no problem."

Both men settled down, but for me, my turbulence had just begun. My restless, shocked eyes searched for her again, but she was nowhere to be seen. She must have gone into the main room where the diners were.

The barman, a smooth bastard, appeared to ask if I wanted a refill.

I nodded and watched blankly as dark vibrant liquid flowed into the glass.

She was here.

She looked even more beautiful than she had been. I'd dreamed of this moment a thousand times and yet, it didn't seem real. I lifted the glass and drained it down.

Sergei gave me a funny look.

Fuck him. What did he know of the sacrifice I'd made? My chest hurt with the memories.

"Will Maxim be present when Luka and Dimitri arrive?" Mikhail asked.

My attention snapped back to my men at the mention of my brother. "Maxim left for Spain this morning."

Both men nodded in understanding. Anytime Maxim was called out of the continent by our father, everyone knew it had to be for something extremely 'delicate'. He would only resurface when it was done to his satisfaction.

I leaned back as far as I could and tried to look into the French seafood restaurant. I had a good view, but I could see no sign of her. I knew she hadn't left yet, so I figured she had to be in one of the private dining rooms.

I started to rise to my feet to casually pass by them, but fell back heavily onto my stool when I saw her come out of the dining area in the company of a man. His arm was possessively snaked around her waist.

As if he owned her.

As if she was fucking his!

I couldn't believe my eyes. I stared at them in disbelief. The irony was too much to bear. I'd walked away from her to save her from the life of a *Bratva* wife, and here she was with the biggest, meanest psychopath in our world. Calling him an animal or a beast was being unfair to animals and beasts. They didn't kill for fun.

This man was a heartless sadist who did his own wet work. Not because he was tight, but because he enjoyed inflicting torture. There were terrible rumors about him, the kind of stuff snuff movies were made of. I didn't usually pay attention to gossip, but there were too many stories from too many credible sources to dismiss. No smoke without fire and there was plenty of poisonous smoke hanging around him.

At first, the shock of seeing *her* with *him* had completely floored me and I couldn't think straight, but as I gathered my wits together, I knew something was not right. They were not opposites who are attracted to each other, they were night and day. They should never be together. I forced myself to focus on her face, and instantly, I felt it.

She *hated* the man who held her as if he owned her.

Her body was stiff with revulsion, her face was tight with a mixture of fear and despair. She was staring straight ahead of her as if she wished she were somewhere else, someone else.

"Tell me that's not Bogdan Litvinenko," I asked, without taking my eyes away from her.

"That's him," Sergei spat out disgustedly, but his voice held a touch of fear.

I ran my hands through my hair and felt as if the blood in my veins had turned to liquid fire. *Damn. What hell on earth have you gotten yourself into, Bianca Russet?*

2

BIANCA

My hand curled tightly around the butter knife I'd stolen from the table. It seemed like a harebrained scheme. How could such a blunt instrument get me out of this mess? Nevertheless, the cold hard metal made me feel as if I had a chance against this monster.

As I stared straight ahead, I couldn't decide who I hated more.

My pathetic father, who had sold me off like chattel, or this disgusting monster, who actually believed he now owned me like some sort of slave. I thought back to the moment my whole life changed.

The image of my father came back to my mind, his face battered, covered in cuts and blood as he'd fallen on his knees to inform me of the barter that had been forced upon him.

"You sold me off to save the bakery?" I asked incredulously.

If he had not been so battered, I'd have thought it was all a sick joke.

"No, not the bakery. I don't give a damn about that," he cried.

"Then what?" I gasped.

Tears filled his eyes and poured down his bloody face.

I stared at him with a mixture of shock and amazement. It was the first time in my life I'd seen him shed tears. He didn't even cry when Mom died.

"You know my history with Mr. Litvinenko. I've been handling goods for him for years."

"Stolen goods, you mean," I corrected automatically.

"Yes, yes, stolen goods," he agreed shamelessly. "But recently, well—uh—I had some troubles along the way so I h-had to ask him, you know—to borrow some cash. I got a little behind in repayments, so he took the opportunity to change our agreement. He says he'll write my debt off in exchange for you. I told him over my dead body, and he said that it was my choice how I wanted it. Whether I was dead or alive, he was going to have you. What do you want me to do?"

I shook my head in disbelief. "What do *I* want you to do?"

"I'll do whatever you want me to do. You decide. I'm happy to sacrifice myself for you. Just say the words and I'll save him the trouble and kill myself."

I closed my eyes and pressed my fingers against my temples. "How much do you owe him, Dad?"

In the dead silence, I snapped my eyes open and stared at my father.

"It doesn't matter how much. The point is he doesn't want the money back."

"How much, Dad?"

For the first time he looked shifty. "Half a million."

"What?" I gasped.

"I mean that's with interest and penalties. I only took about a hundred thousand."

"Oh, sweet Jesus," I muttered, as my knees gave way and I landed in a heap on the cold hard floor of our bakery back room. "We'll have to call the police."

He made a strangled sound of desperation. "The police cannot help. They cannot get to him. He is too powerful. All the top officers and judges are in his back pocket. All it will do is get me arrested for moving stolen goods."

I took a deep breath and laying my hands on the floor, I pushed myself up. I was strong. I could overcome this. I looked into my father's eyes. God only knew why, after all the shit he had pulled on me and Mom, but I still carried a deep sense of loyalty to him. He was a bad father, but he was still my father. The only family I had left.

"We could leave Bridgeport and run away together to a different city. Let him have the bakery and the house. I have some money saved. It will keep us going until we get settled," I said.

"I sold the house and the bakery is worthless," he deadpanned. "I'm sorry, Bee, but you don't know Litvinenko. He will never stop searching for us and when he does find us, he won't be so kind to me ... or you. Now you still have a chance to walk away from all this with little lost. Be good to him and if history is any guide, he will tire of you quickly, and you will walk away with a wardrobe of fine clothes, and more jewelry than the Queen of England wore on her coronation day."

"Do you hear yourself, Dad?" My voice sounded raw and hoarse with his betrayal.

"You think handing you over to him is not hurting me? It's tearing me apart,' he demanded, "But what can I do. We have to somehow find a way to survive this."

"And the only way for us to survive this mess you have created is for me to become his whore?" I asked bitterly.

He flinched. "Don't talk like that, Bianca. You're not a whore. He wants you. He really wants you and he's promised to treat you like a princess. It's not like he's an old man or anything. He's just thirty-nine. I promise it won't last long. He doesn't keep his women for long, but in exchange for a few months with him, you will have access to more money than you could ever need. Play your cards right and you will never need to work another day in your life. I've made you suffer for so long because I couldn't pro-"

"Did I fucking complain?" I screamed at him. "Did I ever, even for one second complain when we went hungry, or when we didn't have enough for me to go with the other kids on a school trip, or when Mom had to wrap presents from the dollar store for my birthdays? How could you do this to me, Dad? How could you destroy me this way?" I couldn't breathe. I felt as if I was suffocating. My own father …

Silence.

We both stared at the other, tears rolling down our faces.

"What can I do?" His voice broke. "Help me, please. Tell me how to fix it. I'll do anything."

"How about we both die?" I asked him.

The expression on his face was incredulous. No matter what happened, or who suffered, my father wanted to carry on living his life.

"What kind of life would it be anyway if you have to live with the fact that you sold your daughter off to a monster like him?" I taunted.

"I have a solution," he said softly.

I stilled, a tender shoot of hope sprouting in my heart.

"Take whatever money you've saved and run away right now. Go somewhere far away, change your name, your history, start again, and never try to come back or contact anybody from this life again … or he will find you."

"And you?" I whispered.

"I'll buy a bottle of sleeping pills and drink it down with a bottle of vodka tonight. I already know exactly what Bogdan has in store for me if I don't give you to him. I've had a good life. It is not a cowardly act to die with dignity. Samurais, the bravest warriors used to do it to avoid shame or betrayal."

The hope inside me died. "That is not a solution."

"It is the only one left, little button ..."

At the use of that old childish pet name for me that I hadn't heard for years, I turned away from him and tried to think. I felt numb and detached from everything. My gaze fell on the assortment of freshly baked cakes and buns I'd just pulled out of the oven. How important it had seemed to me to get them exactly right.

"This might be your last chance to escape," he said to me. "To be free of him. Go now. Before it's too late."

I glanced at the clock. It was five in the morning. The bakery was supposed to be opening in two hours. I thought of our regulars. How they would come for their breakfast and find the closed sign on the door. Except for Sundays, the bakery had never closed once in the last twenty years. Every day without fail, my mother opened it. Even when she was sick, even when she was dying. I had carried on her tradition.

I turned back to face my father. My eyes ran over him, as if he was a stranger. He had taken his hand out of his pocket and for the first time I noticed the thick bandage around his left hand.

"What happened to your hand?' I asked, my voice strangely calm.

"He took off three of my fingers," he said with a shrug, as if he was telling me he'd cut himself while shaving.

A sharp pain hit me so hard I had to clutch my chest. It felt like I'd been stabbed. All I could work up was a whisper, "What?"

He lifted his hand and looked at it emotionlessly. "They're wrapped up in some moist gauze inside a plastic bag and on ice. He'll give them back when I agree to give you to him."

I almost couldn't form the words. The world of ruthless Russian mobsters was so foreign to me I almost couldn't comprehend it. I lived in a world of butter, eggs, flour, and icing sugar. "How does it work? Will you have to go to hospital with your ... fingers?"

He shook his head. "Nah, he has a doctor on standby. He'll attach them for me. After all, I'm still of use to him."

"How much time do you have before ..."

"Don't worry about that," he dismissed this worry. "I'm not going to need them just to wash down some sleeping pills with vodka."

"How much time do you have before those fingers can't be re-attached?" I repeated, my voice hard.

"Six hours."

"Call him now. Tell that monster yes, he can have me. Then go get your damn fingers sewn back on your damn hand."

"But—"

"Do it, Dad," I shouted harshly.

3

BIANCA

https://www.youtube.com/watch?v=MN3x-kAbgFU

We exited the restaurant and there was a glittering ash Maserati awaiting us at the canopied entrance. When one of his men exited the car and came over to hand him the keys, I was instantly on guard. We had arrived in the back of a tinted SUV. I turned to him. "What's going on?" I asked quietly.

"Tonight, it's just the two of us baby," he explained. A low laugh accompanied his words.

The geoduck sashimi and baked lobster I'd forced into me threatened to come up. This was it? The foreplay was over. I had no say in the matter. I wanted to make an excuse. Delay the moment, but what was the point? Today or tomorrow, nothing would change.

He would always be fucking hideous to me.

More than his bloated, sweaty body; large domed forehead, or colorless, thin lips, it was his lashless, dead eyes. There was something inhuman about them. As if he was a different species from me. Like looking into the eyes of a reptile. There was no emotion behind them. Everything warm and alive was prey. When he looked at me, I felt the same way I did when I looked at a black mamba inside a glass enclosure. Instinctive, pure fear.

"Hop in," he said.

I did as I was told. As he rounded the vehicle towards the driver's seat, I was softly tapping the table knife I'd stolen from our table and hidden inside my jeans.

When he'd first noted my plain T-shirt and jeans, there had been a flash of disapproval in his eyes. "I must take you shopping," he had murmured. "A man wears trousers. A beautiful woman should *always* wear a dress."

He slid into the car, closed the door, and started to pull his seatbelt on. "Put yours on," he instructed.

I obeyed and felt a sudden panic to be trapped in such close confines with him. It was as if I was inside the belly of a beast. Even the smell of expensive new leather made me feel nauseous. I forced myself to remember my father's fingers. I was doing this for him. No matter what happens now, at least they had been safely sewn back on.

"What a night this is," he roared suddenly, excitement vibrating like electricity in his voice.

I shivered with fear and revulsion as he switched on the

ignition, the car snarling to life as music blasted into the tight space. Strangely, it was one of my favorite tracks. *Highest in the Room* by Travis Scott. He revved the engine deliberately and I jumped. With a laugh, he let the powerful machine surge forward.

I hugged myself.

We came to a screaming stop at a set of traffic lights, and he turned to peruse his latest acquisition. Turning the music down, he spoke, "My queen, do you know how long I've watched you from afar?"

"What?" I asked in amazement.

"Yes," he confirmed. "I've wanted you from the moment I saw you at your mother's funeral. You didn't cry."

"You were at my mother's funeral?" I whispered. I felt as if I'd dropped down the hole Alice in Wonderland had fallen into.

He nodded slowly. "Why wouldn't I be there? I paid for it. And all her treatments too."

My jaw became slack and I stared at him in shock. "You paid for my mother's treatments."

"In return for your father's house." He made a disgusted face. "But I'll tell you now, if not for my ... desire for you, your useless father would have been crushed like a beetle years ago. But now, it's payback time. For your father and you. So ... let me explain how it will be between us from now on. You will live in my house until I no longer have a need for you. During that time, you will dress how I tell you to, and you will do whatever I tell you to do, no matter how degrading you feel it is, or how repulsed you are by it. In all things, but especially, sexually. I have, shall we say, certain specialized needs. Do I make myself clear?"

I stared at him, speechless, too shocked to even properly comprehend what he was saying, what he was threatening me with. Surely, I had heard wrong.

"I didn't hear your answer," he prompted and there it was again, that unholy light in his dead eyes. He knew I didn't want him and that excited him. Taking by force what didn't want to be taken. He wanted to hurt me. He would enjoy breaking my spirit. He was a monster.

I'd been sold to a freaking monster.

"The lights have changed," I whispered.

Horns began to blare behind us. Unfazed, he brought his hand towards my face and I couldn't help the instinctive move away from him. It only served to fire up his sick amusement. His laughter rang in my ears as he stomped his foot on the gas and we raced forward in a mad frenzy of noise and movement. I shut my eyes to the nightmare that had become my reality. I hoped and prayed that we would crash and end both our lives, or at least, his. A man like him didn't deserve to live.

When the *crash* occurred, it was so sudden, so God-like in its delivery to my prayer that I felt as if my soul left my body.

Something slammed so hard into us that the beast-car lifted off the road and flew into the air. My senses suddenly sharpened and I registered every second as if it was happening in a movie and we were in slow motion. With crystal-clear perception I experienced the car somersaulting, me turning upside down, my body straining against the seatbelt, my right hand desperately clutching the door handle, the grating noise of metal scraping against the road and the sparks that friction produced, before we finally crashed into a lamppost with the sound of an almighty explosion.

As I stared out through the shattered windscreen, I was blinded by the oncoming lights on the opposite side of the road. I didn't feel any pain at all. Just an all-encompassing, astounding, numbing shock ... I was alive.

But so was he.

I heard the monster beside me begin to move and swear in Russian as he tried to extricate himself from the vehicle. While I sat there, in my cramped upside down position, I was too numb to do anything, he found his way out. I closed my eyes and tried to think. I needed to get out. The car could burst into flames.

Suddenly, the sound of a gun rang out and my eyes shot open in terror. I turned my neck towards the side mirror only to see it had been torn off, but through a piece that still hung on I was able to make out a haze of people engaged in vicious combat. This was a new danger that galvanized me into action.

I immediately reached for the seat belt's latch, as I fumbled to set myself free. I could feel the tears of frustration filling my eyes as I fought with the belt and it didn't respond, the buckle, broken by the crash.

I didn't dare scream or make a sound to alert anyone to my presence.

Then at that moment, a masked figure appeared by my side and the door was wrenched open. Terrified, I tried to reach for the knife that I had lodged in my waistband, but it must have fallen out during the crash. Before I could respond, my arm was grabbed and the belt holding me in place was cut away. Before I could fall forward, I was immediately caught and, like a rag doll, dragged out of the wreckage.

"Are you alright?" he asked in a thick Russian accent.

"Yes," I said automatically.

"Good. Come with me," he ordered.

I looked at him as though he were crazy. His face was not only masked, but he was also wearing a baseball cap positioned low enough to shield even his eyes, and I felt as if I was living someone else's life. I should be in my bed now. Sleeping, so I could be up before dawn to start my baking. "Why the hell would I—"

"Because you're not stupid," he shot back impatiently.

In a flash, the truth hit me—anything would be better than the fate Bogdan had in mind for me. Everything from then on was a blur as I was dragged through a flurry of rapid activity. Soon, I was inside on the backseat of an SUV just as another shot rang out. The whole earth seemed to shudder at the release and so did I, as I looked around in fright. The SUV zoomed off with me and the three masked men inside it.

We went through the Holland tunnel and out of the state as I realized that we must be heading to New Jersey.

None of the men spoke to me, but neither did they try to

restrain me in any way. They had taken their caps and masks off. They were bulky, thickly muscled men, covered in tattoos with military-styled haircuts, and hard, determined faces.

"W-why have I been taken?" I stuttered.

The one closest to me replied, "Have no fear. We will not harm you."

"Where are you taking me?"

"You will be safe," he replied.

Usually, I was an even-tempered person, mild even, but with all the incredible goings-on of the last twenty-four hours, my nerves were shot to pieces. My temper flared like acid through my system. "How am I to know that when I don't know who the hell any of you are?"

He turned away from me, neither intimidated nor the slightest bit bothered by my outburst.

With a scowl, I placed my head in my hands and tried to think. What the hell was happening? Had I become a pawn in some *Bratva* feud? How was I to extricate myself from this mess? What would happen to my father? With the exception of my best friend, Aldie, I made a vow then, that if I were somehow lucky enough to come out of all of this alive ... I would never have anything to do with any Russians again for the rest of my life.

I lifted my head and stole a glance at them.

They showed no interest in me at all. They were all staring

straight ahead or glancing at the rear-mirror to make sure we were not being followed.

Slowly, my hand inched towards the door handle. I waited … my stomach twisted into tight knots until the car came to a stop at a red light. I took a deep breath, and pushing away the memory of the gun they had fired earlier, I pulled with all my strength at the door latch.

The door refused to budge. I lost my shit then and banged on it with my fists. I felt angry, frustrated and utterly helpless.

The men didn't move an inch.

When I turned to see the bored looks on their faces at my little temper tantrum, my heart fell. Exhausted, I settled into the seat and momentarily accepted my fate. Even my butter knife was gone. I would just save my energy until it would be time once again, to fight back.

Perhaps it was the route they followed, but after a while, there was very little illumination for me to figure out where we were headed. Finally, we arrived at the imposing gates of what looked to be a very huge estate.

Beautiful big trees loomed on either side of the driveway. As we arrived at the house, I couldn't help but gasp at the grandiosity of the massive beautifully lit fountain.

Water spewed out of the mouths of four stone figures, a lion, an ox, an eagle, and a deer. A Greek-style statue of a magnificent man with wild hair stood amidst them. And the house that it sat behind was like something out of a Hollywood movie. It reminded me of The Great Gatsby. Enormous and lit up ... it shone like a jewel in the night.

The car came to a stop and I watched, alert as two of the men jumped out of the car like large cats and came over to my side to escort me.

To my surprise, they stayed on either side of me, but made no attempt to use any force to get me out.

I had never been so confused in my life. "Where am I?" I asked.

"Hopefully, someone will soon address that question for you," one of them said dryly.

I put my foot on the ground and tried to stand, but my knees gave way.

The men reacted with lightning speed. They grabbed my forearms and held on until I found my strength again.

"Thanks. I'm alright now," I said awkwardly.

Both men let go of me. With all the adrenaline running through my system, I hadn't felt any pain, but now I could feel the aches and pains all over my body. Especially my back. I felt like a crumpled wreck as we started walking towards the house.

A heavy lion head knocker sat on the door. I kept my gaze on it. I didn't know what would happen next and I should be afraid, but for some strange reason, I wasn't. Before we could get to the door, the knocker moved backwards.

The door had been opened from the inside by a man.

My blood froze over. I simply couldn't believe my eyes. Perhaps my eyes and current state of disorientation were playing tricks on me. The light was behind him and I couldn't be absolutely sure.

Then he moved and the light fell on his face.

4

BIANCA

https://www.youtube.com/watch?v=Bx5IeegLTY8

I stared at him incredulously, not knowing what to feel as my gaze was met and held by the man I wasn't good enough for, the man who'd broken my heart a lifetime ago.

He seemed different than when I knew him. The carefree young man was gone, in his place was a man older, harder, sadder, with secrets in his eyes.

He stepped aside to allow me into the house.

I did not move an inch. I couldn't. "You?" I gasped.

"Yes, it's me." His gaze searched my face and body intently. "Are you alright? Do you have any injuries at all?"

Injuries? This man broke my heart. I shook my head in a daze.

"Come inside and we'll talk."

His voice sounded exactly the same. Hearing his voice again was a different kind of shock. It brought back all the pain of the past. I had poured out my heart to him and he had walked away without even the courtesy of a goodbye. Even the worst kind of jerk would have sent a break-up text. One day, his account was alive with a green symbol and the next it came up with a message telling me IvanTheGreat did not exist. I'd felt so confused and in such a state of denial, I had contacted Support to say there was a problem with the Ivan-TheGreat account. They told me the account had been deleted by the user. Then I called his number. It was as dead as his account.

"Ivan the Great, my ass," I muttered. "Go talk to yourself. I have nothing to say to you." I turned around to walk away and realized the men and the SUV were gone. I'd been so shocked by his appearance I hadn't even noticed what was going on around me. No-one remained to stop me, but where would I go? I didn't even know where I was. Besides, there were too many unanswered questions. Questions about whether Bogdan was still alive, and other old questions that had been burning in my brain ever since he disappeared without a trace.

I whirled around to face him.

He stood, watching me intently, his face carefully wiped of all expression.

"How the hell did you ... no wait ... why did you take me away from him?"

"I heard what happened ... with your father."

My eyes slid away in shame, but I held my gaze to the door's frame and went on. "And so you just decided to what? Rescue me?" Hurt made my tone belittling and mocking. If he had been anyone else, I would have been kissing his feet with gratitude. Instead, I was being an ungrateful bitch.

"I saw you in the restaurant. He put his hand on you. I couldn't take it." His words were clipped, his tone curt.

Something inside me, something I'd held on to with all my might snapped. My God, if I stayed here any longer I'd become a sniveling fool and start imagining he had feelings for me when he had clearly shown he had none.

I turned away and started to walk away, but I'd only gone a few steps, before I stopped, swiveled around and marched back up to him. "What's with the Russian guards?" I waved my hand in a wide arc. "And this house? Weren't you an accounting major at NYU?"

"I graduated," he responded.

"I know that," I snapped. Then I shut my eyes to get a hold of myself.

He went on, "The 'Russian guards' work for my father. I sought out their help because they are damn good at what they do."

"You said you're from Spain," I said. "You never mentioned anything about Russia." Ivan the Great suddenly made sense. "You're Russian, aren't you?"

"Come in, Bianca," he urged. "I'll answer all the questions you need me to, but it's the middle of the night right now."

I swallowed hard. Jesus, I *wanted* to go in with him. All the more reason I shouldn't. I stayed put where I was. "What about Bogdan? I heard gunshots. Is he dead?"

"Unfortunately, no." He frowned. "Killing him would have started a war. Even doing what I did was already bad enough, but when I saw you with him, I didn't think. I acted on instinct."

I felt fear clutch at my heart. He was still out there and almost certainly fuming that his prey had been snatched right from under his nose. "What happens now?"

"Now that you're missing he'll go after everyone and everywhere you could possibly return to. He will not stop until he finds you."

It hit me like a ton of bricks. I slapped my hand on my mouth. "How can I remain here in safety when everyone else I love could be in danger? My father? Aldie?"

"I've sent people to keep an eye on the both of them. Your father is nowhere to be found at the moment, but we have eyes on Aldie. If there is any danger at all, we'll step in."

I searched his gray eyes. They were so familiar. I must have seen them a million times in my dreams. "Why did you do this?"

"I couldn't let him take you. Not him," he said, running his hand through his thick dark hair.

I scoffed. "That is incredibly hard to believe."

"Believe it or not, it's the truth." Then he turned and walked into the house.

I remained outside, my gaze on the luxurious foyer, inviting me to come and forget the harshness of my ordeal. *Don't go in. It's a trap. You'll burn your wings. You know nothing about him. What you remember is a mirage. Worse still, you'll go and fall in love with him all over again. Then he'll just walk away ...* Everything my head was saying was true, but I couldn't exactly stand out here all night.

I found myself moving over the threshold and shutting the door behind me.

The house was simply magnificent. But I couldn't fully appreciate all the beauty and luxury as I looked around. I thought a stern butler or housekeeper would appear to tell me where to go but no one did, so I wandered to the right and found what was certainly just one of many living areas in the house.

A television screen bigger than any I'd ever seen, hung from a wall. Probably custom. The furniture, expensive carpets and art pieces, all dripped of surreal wealth and it started to dawn on my shocked, disorientated brain that he was not just another ordinary accounting student who had become a regular at our bakery years ago.

I followed a corridor that opened out to all these fabulous rooms until I stood at the threshold of a massive minimalist kitchen. The ceilings were lofty and it was done up in pure white. The only color in it was a bunch of very yellow bananas hanging from a gleaming metal stand.

It all looked so beautifully perfect, a sigh rose up from deep inside me. This was the exact kitchen I had always dreamed of. Here, I could create little mouthfuls of heaven. I walked into it like someone in a trance.

"Do you want something to eat?" his voice asked from behind me.

I turned around to see him standing at the entrance. "No," I responded, and watched him. Now that my brain felt slightly less scrambled, I could see him better. Dressed simply in a pair of dark slacks and a white shirt, he looked even more dashing than the man I'd met two years earlier.

I still remember, the first time I saw this man, I'd been so utterly stunned by his beauty, the stainless tongs I'd been holding had slipped out of my suddenly nerveless hands. Confused and red-faced I'd ducked down under the counter to retrieve them and banged my head hard on my way back up.

"Are you alright?" he'd asked, his voice poured out of him like melted chocolate. It swirled around me deliciously. Something in his eyes sparkled in a way that made it hard for me to breathe. I had never met anyone who carried a storm in their eyes before.

My head had been thumping like there would be no tomorrow, but I'd nodded vigorously since I'd been struck dumb. Like a love-struck teenager, I'd wrapped up his order clumsily, my fingers shaking so much, I couldn't do up the bow and had to leave the ribbons hanging over the sides of the box like two flags of defeat.

He'd thanked me, a lop-sided smile on his face, his gorgeous eyes dancing, and left a massive tip.

I had to wait two weeks more for the drop-dead gorgeous stranger to come by once again.

But I wasn't the infatuated fool anymore. I hardened my face. "I want a phone," I said. "To call Aldie."

"Sure," he responded, pulling his phone from his pocket and coming towards me.

My breath caught in my throat as he came closer. *You better calm down,* I cautioned myself. *Oh, no, we're not doing that again.*

Unaware of the effect he was having on me, he held out his phone to me.

I swallowed and steeled myself. I was almost too scared to take it ... too scared to touch him. Carefully, so our fingers did not touch I gingerly took it from him.

"The password is 2359," he said softly.

I tapped the numbers then realized I couldn't actually remember Aldie's number. I looked up at him in dismay. "I can't remember her number. Would you have a computer or laptop, so I can access my email account?"

He smiled, that wonderful magician's smile of his. That was what I used to call him. He could make a simple picnic into a slice of heaven or a boring study session into the most exciting encounter. He was always conjuring rabbits out of a hat, until he did his last trick and disappeared into thin air. To my horror, my face heated up with such acute awareness of how it was between us that a delicious tingle went all the way down to my spine.

"That won't be necessary," he said. "I have Aldie's number."

I stared at him in astonishment. "You have Aldie's number?"

He shrugged casually. "You never know when you might need to call someone. It's saved as Stinky."

My eyebrows shot up at the nickname. "Stinky?"

"She was always a snippy, snappy thing back then." His smile had gone into dangerous territory, the stormy gray eyes sparkling like trouble in the sunshine.

I wasn't interested in that kind of trouble. I got myself firmly back on track. Swinging my gaze away from him, hit her number, and said coolly, "She's going to kill you if she ever finds out."

"She won't if you don't tell her."

I walked away from him when Aldie picked up. "It's Bianca," I said quickly.

"Where are you? Are you okay?" she demanded.

My smile was bitter. I hadn't told her about Bogdan yet. She had no idea just how much my life had changed from the early hours of the morning when I'd left the apartment we both shared to go to the bakery.

"It's a long story," I said with a heavy sigh and walked towards a tall window.

5

LEVAN

https://www.youtube.com/watch?v=UJ8RBj_PoKQ

I watched her standing at the window and I still couldn't believe she was really here. I could feel my heart beating fast with a strange sense of fear and excitement. I was aware of just what I'd gotten myself involved in. War was what I had unleashed. Bogdan's enterprise may not be as reputable and distinguished as ours – but his army of thieves, smugglers, hired killers all over the city – would be enough to cause some serious damage. I knew there would be collateral damage, I might even be part of that body count, but I was prepared to risk it. Nothing and no one could dissuade me from the course I was on now.

I felt a presence behind me and turned. I jerked my head to the side to indicate he should follow me to the corridor.

"Bogdan just went on a rampage," Sergei reported once we

were just outside the room. "He just gunned down two of his own men."

I paused in thought. That meant he still hadn't been able to figure out who'd taken Bianca.

"He'll keep going until he finds her," Sergei said.

I didn't need the reminder. I turned to look at Bianca. Her back was turned to me and I couldn't hear her voice, but it was the closest she'd ever felt to me. She had always seemed too good for me. Unattainable. But as the seconds ticked by and with the sound of Sergei's breathing in my ear, I could feel it happening all over again. The distance was once again widening, my grip on her loosening ...

There was a reason I had walked away two years earlier, and it was still valid. So just what was I doing?

I turned my gaze back to him, a frown on my face. The conclusion from his statement was clear to the both of us. Either I kept her hidden and allowed the bodies to pile up, or I give her up and stopped the bloodshed.

"How far are you willing to go?" Sergei asked, staring at me intently. It was as though he were trying to read my mind.

"Did Anne return?"

"Yeah, the guys just dropped her off," he responded.

"Have her prepare a room for Bianca, and something to eat."

"Which room?"

"I want to keep an eye on her. The one next to mine. Tell

Gloria to make her a Spanish omelet and to make it spicy. Bianca likes it hot."

Obviously, he didn't see the wisdom in my actions. His lips snapped closed as he nodded.

I could see Gloria, our housekeeper coming from the other end of the corridor. She would take care of Bianca's needs now. I had some serious thinking to do. I tapped Sergei's shoulder consolingly as I walked past.

6

BIANCA

Levan had done another disappearing act and I was shown to my room by the housekeeper, Gloria, a tiny, soft-spoken woman dressed in a high-necked black dress. She had white hair and rosy cheeks. She behaved as if nothing was out of the ordinary. As if I was simply a guest of her employer.

It would be unnecessary to say that the room was beautiful. Classy soft gray walls with accents of white. The bed was huge and smelt of lavender, but I didn't even sit on it to try it out. I felt so soiled. As soon as she closed the door quietly behind her, I rushed to the bathroom and began to strip. I got to the massive cubicle that would have fit ten people, turned the shower on, and waited until it was the right temperature before I stepped into the glorious cascade.

I turned my face up and let the water wash away the whole day.

My head was jumbled with all kinds of thoughts. Would

Bogdan think it was my father who had busted me out? No. My father didn't have those kind of resources or the guts to do something like that. Would Bogdan hurt my father now, since I'd been taken? No, he would probably try to use him as some kind of bartering advantage. What would happen to the bakery? Nothing. And the staff? I would have to call them in the morning. No, I couldn't do that without letting Bogdan know that I was alive and well ... able to make calls. God, what a mess.

The heat from the water felt good on my sore body. I massaged the strained muscles in my shoulder blades and my back. By tomorrow, they would probably be even stiffer.

As my body began to unwind, I closed my eyes and thought of Levan. I never thought I would ever see him again. For at least a year, I looked at tall men with black hair and imagined it was him, but it was never him. So eventually, I stopped looking, stopped expecting those men to be him. It felt as if I was in a dream, but circumstances had made his appearance in my life, a surreal nightmare.

My mind returned to the past. I remembered how he had charmed himself into my life. Aldie and I had been invited to a poolside party off campus hosted by one of the rich kids from her English department. It had seemed a strange invite, because the girl had snubbed me in the past and she had asked Aldie to bring 'that girl you always hang out with.'

As soon as we arrived, we saw Levan waiting for us at the stone steps. Like some kind of hero-god, he rose and began to walk towards us. My stomach knotted and my mouth became dry. I got so nervous at the prospect of not making a fool of myself again, I walked right into the water fountain.

Then, in an even more humiliating effort to save myself, I grabbed and dragged him in with me. We made a spectacular splash. There must have been a hundred or so students milling around the grounds that saw us fall in. While I contemplated drowning with shame, he came up, roaring with laughter. I watched him as though in a trance. I think I was already half in love with him then.

But even if I hadn't been utterly infatuated, this was the beauty about Levan. Unlike me, he seemed devoid of concerns or problems. Carefree as a bird, he threw caution to the winds and lived every moment as if it was his last. He dragged me out of my reserved, insecure shell and made me do things I would never have dared. He made my life magical ... and then hell, when he vanished without a trace.

I opened my eyes and turned off the shower. Levan still had the same smile, but his eyes were different. From what I could gather so far, he was now deeply involved in the brutal world of the *Bratva*. Right now, and either-way, I would ensure that Levan would be the least of my problems. I walked out of the stall and wrapped myself in the fluffy towel that had been neatly folded and left on a round pillar style marble table. As I luxuriated in its softness, I wondered just how rich Levan really was.

He had always 'smelled' of money and had that easy confidence of rich people. I guess knowing you can buy your way out of any kind of trouble must be a great feeling. Still, there was never any real indication I could point to. He never wore designer gear, drove up in a gold lambo, or flashed his money around.

Maybe if I'd had enough time, but he'd just come and gone like the wind ... unpredictable and untraceable. My gaze took in the obviously expensive big slabs of dark marble surrounding me. This much money was quite over-whelming for me. Before Mom started the bakery, I was one of those children who went to bed hungry as the month got closer to the end because Dad had gambled away his wages.

I walked back into the bedroom ... and *stopped* at the sight of food. Walking over to it, I quickly realized what I was looking at: Spanish omelet. Once I'd told Levan, it was my favorite meal. The only problem was it was a lie. From a girl who had been so desperate to connect with him on any level she was willing to do almost anything. When Levan had mentioned he loved the dish, the lie had fallen from my lips without me even thinking about it.

I could see that my dirty clothes were gone, probably already spinning in a washing machine, so I stayed in the towel I was wrapped in. Lying on a cream daybed, I inputted his password and dialed Aldie again.

She answered on the first ring. "Everything okay?" she asked urgently.

"Yeah, I'm fine. Are you alright?"

"I'm not the one who has been in a car crash and being held, location unknown."

"Do you have any news?" I asked quickly.

"Um … yeah. You're hundred percent sure his surname is Ivankov?"

"Well, not a hundred percent, but that's what I saw on a document lying on the kitchen counter as I passed."

"Uh … but he's never mentioned his surname before?"

I sighed. "You were there too. Do you remember him giving anything away?"

"You have a point there. He was always more than a bit mysterious. Well, if Ivankov really is his surname, then I don't know what to say."

I sat up. "Why?"

"Well, his family is one of the most successful Russian *Bratva* families, if not *the* most successful."

"What? He said his father lived in Spain."

"That's not exactly a lie. His father does live there, half the year. He's the billionaire head of a conglomerate that seems to have all the politicians in America on speed dial. He has more photos with Putin than I have with my mom."

"Putin?"

"Yup, the President of Russia."

"I know that. I was expressing surprise."

"By the way his brother, Maxim is … umm … fierce."

"What do you mean?"

"Anatoly showed me a picture of him online. By God I'd pay him to take me hostage."

"Aldie ..."

"Sorry, sorry. What can I do? I'm just a hot-blooded woman. Anyway, to get back to the story, I called up Anatoly, and you know he's a know-it-all when it comes to the Russian community. The Ivankovs basically run New York when it comes to the Russian *Bratva*. They seem to have been accused of everything under the sun except none of them have ever been caught. They say his father is named *The Ghost* because even when he is there you don't see him. They say he also has the American judicial system in his pocket."

"Wow," I whispered.

"There's quite a lot of info about him and his older brother, but Anatoly says he doesn't know much about Levan. However, he does think Levan might be in training and have recently been left in charge of their business activities while Maxim is out of town. Mind you, that's just him guessing because there doesn't seem too much known about any of them. Most people don't even know what Levan looks like. I think he must hire someone to scrub the net for him. I had to go to page six of Google to find one grainy photo of him when he was in his teens."

"What kind of—"

I was interrupted by a sudden knock to the door. I thought it would be my clothes, so I quickly ended the call with Aldie and was about to rise and answer it when the door was rudely pushed open. It startled me, especially as Levan loomed in the doorway.

I instantly shot to my feet, only to realize I was semi-naked, so I plopped back down and tried to achieve some level of dignity. "Why can't you wait until you're invited in?" I said haughtily.

I thought he would turn away for courtesy's sake, instead his eyes ran over me in a way that made my heart seize. My lips parted to sound another complaint but no words left my mouth.

"I need my phone," he said into the strange, thick silence.

I looked at the device in my hand as if it had suddenly turned into a dead rat. Ah yes, his phone. Of course, he needed it, but I couldn't let it go … I needed to be in touch with Aldie in case she heard from my dad. "I can't get up," I said stupidly. I swear, I must have suffered brain injury in the crash, because I was saying the stupidest things.

He began to head towards me.

At his approach, my stomach did a double flip. "Don't come here," I warned. "I'm not dressed."

"Just throw it to the bed," he said, his tone somewhat bored.

This aggravated me and gave my lob extra oomph as I did as I was told. The phone bounced off the bed and landed on the floor.

My breath hitched at my unintentional brattiness.

He narrowed his gaze at me.

I couldn't bring myself to apologize. After all, he had caused me far, far more pain and suffering than having to bend to retrieve a phone.

He picked up the phone and without even a glance my way, he turned around to exit the room.

"I know your family is huge with the *Bratva*," I heard myself saying.

He stopped in his tracks and turned to face me. "My family *is* the *Bratva*," he corrected softly.

It took me a few moments to get my mouth to work again. "Does that mean you'll be able to help me? To handle Bogdan, I mean?"

"What sort of help are you looking for?"

I had grown up with a very good idea of the *Bratva* and their dealings in Bridgeport were constant headlines, so it wasn't too difficult to surmise that the only help that would be good enough to keep Bogdan from exacting revenge on me and my dad would either be his own death, or a super long prison sentence. And I wasn't even sure about the prison sentence. Still, I wanted to know what Levan would say. Perhaps he would be able to shine some light on an option that I may have missed. "What kind of help will get him off my back?"

"Are you ready to take his life?" he asked so casually he could have as well been asking if I liked a certain brand of cereal.

I definitely did not have a response to that.

He turned and exited the room.

https://www.youtube.com/watch?v=ZSM3wɪv-A_Y

"I'm leaving," she stated from the doorway.

I'd had a bad night and I was seated in the sun room and on my third cup of strong coffee.

The rays of morning sun turned her hair to spun gold. Bianca Russet was beautiful first thing in the morning.

I put the cup down on the table. "Where are you going?" I asked gently.

"I don't know. I just know I can't stay here forever."

"It's been a night," I pointed out.

"I can't keep hiding here. I have to find a way to resolve this mess. Somehow."

I leaned back against the chair and gazed at her. She would never know how much pleasure I got from simply looking at her. Her youth, her beauty, her innocence. "And how are you planning on doing that?"

She pressed her hands together, her face full of determination. "I don't know, but I'll figure it out. I'll find my dad and we'll go away, far away. Somewhere he can't find us."

"You don't know the kind of resources Bogdan has."

"I have to risk it. You said it yourself that beyond killing him, you won't be able to help me. I don't want anyone's blood, not even his on my hands, so I have to figure it out somehow."

"It's already too late for that sentiment," I said.

Her gorgeous, ocean-blue eyes widened. "W-what do you mean?"

"He's already gunned down two of his own men. They've still been unable to find you, so they'll keep falling victim to his ... annoyance until he does."

Her body visibly trembled.

I was instantly sorry I'd been so brutal. I was trying to make her understand the gravity of the situation, but I didn't take into consideration her innocence. She wasn't used to the ruthlessness of my world. I shot to my feet. "Bianca?"

Tears filled her eyes. "How can—how can he just kill people like that?"

"That's the way this ... my world works."

She stared at me in horror. "Your world? That means—does that mean you've killed humans too?"

I felt my chest constrict. This horror was exactly what I tried to protect her from.

"Answer me," she cried.

"I haven't yet, but I would if I needed to." I folded my arms across my chest. The truth was I wanted to give excuses, to explain that this was the world I'd been born into. To kill or to be killed, and there was little else I'd ever known. The only time I'd contemplated breaking free, leaving to chart another course, was when I first met her. The desire had gripped me and I had begun to lay down my plans, then something happened and it had slammed me right back into the clutches of my brutal world. I knew then there was no escape for me, but I had no right to drag her into my hell.

"Then you're no better than Bogdan, are you?" she accused, her voice raw with emotion.

Something cold slithered through me. "I'm not."

For a moment, I could see that she was taken back by the bile in my tone.

"I'm sorry," she said softly. "I have no right to judge you."

"You don't."

She shook her head. "I need to find my father. Thank you for your help." She turned around to leave.

I watched to see if she was serious. I stood there until she got to the foyer. Fuck, she was serious. I ran to the foyer. "If you leave," I called out. "There will be no getting out of this.

I can assure you of one thing ... by the time Bogdan is through with you, you will be mentally and physically scarred forever."

"Well if I don't, it's only a matter of time before he hurts Aldie and my dad. So I don't have much of a choice, do I?"

"He won't hurt them," I assured her. "At least, not while he doesn't know where you are, or who you are with. Hurting them has no value to him other than to get you back, but it will only be worth anything if you're actually aware that he will hurt them. A message is only one when it is received."

"So what should I do?" she cried desperately. "What the fuck should I do?"

"Stay," I said. "At least for now, I'll protect you and ensure that Aldie is alright. I told you last night, I have men right now watching her."

"How long?" she whispered.

"Until Maxim returns. He is the head of our operation and until he gives a go ahead, we cannot go full throttle on this war. We have already started it and for that, the consequences are already dire enough. Anymore and it might all get out of hand. By then, it might be too late to contain any of this.

"And when does he return? Your brother."

"He'll be back in less than a week. Until then, we'll keep an eye on your father and Aldie, and afterwards, see how we can resolve things with Bogdan. But until then, we can't add any more fuel to this fire."

She took a moment to ruminate on the lie I had just spun.

I was the one in complete charge of New York while Maxim controlled our international dealings. But I needed time to figure out everything. I wasn't giving her up this time. I was prepared to do whatever it took to keep her. Even kill for her if need be. No price was too high, but I needed time to lay my plans.

"Is this your new number?" Aldie asked.

"Yeah, Levan got me a prepaid, so I can keep in touch with you, but like before please don't give this number to anyone or even tell anyone that you've heard from me."

"What if your dad calls looking for you?

I gripped the phone harder. "Especially, not if Dad contacts you. Just say you haven't heard from me and pretend to be worried and confused."

"Your bakery is closed. When is all this going to be resolved?"

"I have no idea," I muttered.

"What do you mean you have no idea?" she demanded worriedly.

"He says in a week when his brother returns from Spain, but I can't see how this is going to end."

"Why does he need his brother to resolve this?"

"Look, I'm actually in the dressing room of some high-end boutique right now, but I just wanted to call you and quickly give you my new number."

"Hang on, what are you doing at a high-end boutique?"

"I'm supposed to be getting some clothes, but ..." I picked up a pair of black pants that a saccharine sweet assistant had hung on the rail in the dressing room, and looked at the price tag. It read $2,680.00. "Good God!" I muttered, as it fell from my hands. I stared down at it as though it were a poisonous snake.

"What is it?" Aldie asked urgently.

"Nothing, just saw the price for a pair of pants."

"Bianca," Levan's voice suddenly sounded from outside the dressing room.

It made me jump in alarm. I held onto my chest at the painful slam, and my eyes tightened shut at the headache that had been laying its roots in my head since last night.

"Bianca," Levan called again.

"Yeah?" I managed to croak out.

"You've been in there a while, are you okay?"

"Uh, yeah—I just uh—I'm fine. I'll be out soon." I looked down at the shirt and jeans I'd been wearing since the previous day. They were clean, but they were both torn, and I knew I could get away with torn jeans, they were all the rage now. But I needed at least one outfit to change into so, I began to quickly sort through the rack. I found a light sweater top. The price. A whopping $2,500! Unbelievable.

I looked at the ordinary woolen fabric with contempt. It's real worth I was sure was nothing more than $90. I kept going and eventually, came across a black and white striped top. $900. Totally not worth it, but it would have to do. I'd have to grit my teeth and reimburse him when this whole mess was over.

I immediately slipped my hands through the sleeves, but when I tried to pull up the zipper behind me, I had to gasp at the pain that shot up my back. My heart once again sank at the thought I would need some help. Perhaps I could get the saccharine sweet girl to do it up.

I moved, breathless to the door to see if she was anywhere close. "Hello?" I called out my voice a whisper.

No response came, as Miss Saccharine had locked the door of the shop when we came so no one else could come in.

With a sigh, I headed back out into the sitting area to see Levan going through his phone.

"I'll take this one," I said. "But can you help me with the zipper, please?"

"What about the rest?" he asked with a slight frown.

"Unnecessary. Just this one will do."

His gaze ran over me. "You'll need more than that. To start with, it's getting colder."

His intense gaze made the hairs on my body stand on end.

"This is just for today. I can ask Aldie to post some clothes for me."

"She will not be able to get in touch with you."

My brows furrowed. "Why?"

"Bogdan's men will have their eyes on her. Any contact with her will immediately expose the fact that we have you."

I stared at him. My thinking still seemed muddled as if all my faculties were not right yet, after the crash.

"The situation is more severe than you think," he said. "Get some more clothes. And shoes. Socks, underwear, the whole bit."

"Well, I can't get anything from this store. It's all so damn expensive."

"Don't concern yourself. I'll cover it," he said.

"You know me better than that, Levan. I can't let you spend all this money on me. You've already done enough by rescuing me. Can we go to a cheaper store nearby? There are some Ross stores not too far away and we can—"

"We came here for a reason, Bianca. It's private."

My face tightened with the thought of how much in debt I was to him.

With a sigh, he stood. "I'll get Evelyn to send everything over to the house. Let's go."

"The last time I told you I liked you, you disappeared for two years," I blurted out.

He stopped in his tracks. "I didn't disappear. I was shot. Four times, in the chest. I was unconscious for nearly a month."

"What?"

He began to slip the buttons out of his shirt.

I had long frozen over in shock.

He held my gaze, and unblinking, he held his shirt open.

I saw them then.

Four pigmented, textured dips marked the skin on his lower abdomen and chest, one of the dips looked to be a mere inch away from his heart.

I lifted my eyes to him in horror. "How the hell are you still alive?" I breathed

Time stopped—the world outside the plush cream and gold waiting room fell away. There was no one else, nothing else but us left in the universe. All the worries and troubles were gone. Hypnotized, I stared into his eyes. I watched in fascination as his pupils grew until they were so big there was almost no more color in them. It was wonderful to see.

I didn't know how long we stood there just staring into each other's eyes, or for how long we stayed frozen in this beautiful, intense bubble where it was just the two of us, but I could have stayed there forever.

I jumped with shock when one of his men suddenly burst into the room. Disoriented, I could only stare as he muttered rapid Russian to Levan.

As Levan listened, he quickly buttoned his shirt.

When the man stopped speaking, he replied curtly in Russian, and the man ran back out.

"What's wrong?" I asked my stomach tight with anxiety.

"Bogdan knows I have you," he said.

I snapped out of my dazed state. "How did he find out you had me?"

"The very thing I intend to find out," he snarled with a scowl. "Come on, we need to leave, now."

I turned around. "Could you help me zip this up?"

He grabbed the end of the zipper, but a tiny part of one of his fingers briefly grazed my skin.

I shuddered at the frisson of electricity that shot into my body.

"Are you alright?" he asked as he pulled the zipper up.

"Yes," I mumbled.

"Done," he said. "Let's go."

I turned around and grabbed his hand. "Why didn't you contact me?" I asked urgently. "When all of this happened, why did you shut me out? I thought you'd—thrown me away. That you saw my message and— decided I was not good enough."

His gaze looked filled with anguish. "We'll talk about this later."

But I couldn't let it go. It had been too painful, the longing, the hurt, the regret. I lifted myself up on my tiptoes and took his lips in a quick kiss.

All I needed was to taste him, a privilege I'd never had and dreamed about incessantly, for years. No matter what happened now, I just had to know if the reality would match the fantasy. If it didn't, then I would know I had made it all up in my head and I could stop comparing him to all other men just to find them lacking. If it did, then I would die knowing I had tasted my greatest dream. Something not many people get to do in their lifetimes.

Our first kiss and I stole it from him. In a moment that should have been full of panic and fear. But I wasn't afraid. I had been waiting for his kiss and his touch for years. I felt calm and sure of myself as I lost myself to the moment.

He tasted of coffee, but that soon washed away. My tongue found his and I felt desire so potent that it was like a snake coiling in the pit of my stomach. The sensation took my breath away.

I thought he would push me away, instead, he stilled. I held onto his shoulders to balance myself and angled my head for a longer kiss, the memory of which I wanted engraved on my heart. When I pulled my lips away from his and started to move away, he grabbed me and slammed me hard against his body. In the next instant, he covered my mouth with his and ...

Freaking hell—I saw stars.

I'd imagined kissing him more times than was possible to count, but I had never once imagined it like this. His tongue danced with mine, sucking and teasing with a fervency that set my blood on fire.

I forgot about the danger of Bogdan waiting to reclaim me. All I could feel was him. His fresh scent of grapefruit, sea, and musk, the burn of his skin against my face as he kissed me hard and rough. To my shock, he was every bit as desperate as I was. Every bit as impatient and insatiable. As though he too, had been waiting for this moment his whole life.

Suddenly, he tore himself away from me. He now seemed like a stranger, a man I'd never seen before. The affable, fun guy gone. Here was an animal breathing hard, as if trying to control itself. Even his stormy eyes were different. They were blazing with lust.

For a moment, he stood in front of me fighting with himself while I stared at him. I knew then that the story of my life would be forever split cleanly in two. The me that had been before Levan had kissed me, and the me after.

When his gaze fixed on mine, I knew he was in control again.

I lifted my hand and let my knuckles brush down the side of his face.

"We need to leave now," another one of his men shouted in English.

I didn't even realize anyone had come into the room.

Levan pulled away and turned around to face him.

"Looks like Bogdan's men are on their way here," he said.

I looked between the worry on both men's faces, but was

still too muddled from the kiss to fully digest the danger of the moment.

Levan turned to me. "Let's go," he said. He held out his hand.

I hesitated as I stared at the strong limb ... I hesitated because despite this torment of need and desire I had nursed for him from the day I met him, there would be consequences to being with him. He lived in a world where no one grew old.

If I took that hand ... how far would we go before I had to once again, let it go?

"Bianca," he called.

I felt like my insides were trembling. Then I grabbed his hand, a hold so tight, my knuckles showed white as we hurried out of the store.

A FEW MINUTES later and we were zooming away in his SUV.

"My dad ..." I muttered.

The man I had dreamed about was seated by my side and my hand was still tightly held in his and it shouldn't have been the happiest day of my life ... but as we sped away, all I could see in my mind's eyes was the image of my dad with his bandaged hand and sweet, laughing Aldie.

I turned to him in despair. "Now that he knows, he'll get to my dad, and Aldie, won't he?"

"On the contrary,' he said. "They are safer. Now that he knows your father had nothing to do with it, he will be safe for a while. At least, while he has the value of being a bargaining chip. Same with Aldie, we have a lot of eyes on her. We don't want to pull her out from her workplace, so that he will think this whole thing is business related. But at the tiniest sign of danger, we'll move in to protect her. I promise you."

I tried to find reassurance in his words, but life had a way of kicking me in the teeth when I least expected it.

9

LEVAN

I sat at my desk, but my swivel chair was turned towards the window as I stared blankly out of it. I laboriously and meticulously went over all the steps in my plan. I kept trying to foresee and imagine every possible mishap that could happen along the way. I cursed silently when Yuri interrupted my contemplation by slipping into my study.

"What is it?" I asked, turning around to face him.

"He's kidnapped Sarah Dale and one of her grandchildren and he's requesting a meeting," he announced.

I went still. Shit. I hadn't expected the situation to deteriorate so quickly. That Bogdan would dare to take us on in this way was incredible. There was only one conclusion. I was dealing with a mad man. "He's taken the Solicitor General?"

Yuri nodded in response.

Folding my arms, I leaned into the leather chair. I knew Bogdan bordered on insane, but it was clear now that years of debauchery and brutality had made him completely crazy. "Which one of her grandchildren did he kidnap?"

"The boy," he replied. "He just turned nine."

"When and where does he want to meet?"

"Today at 6pm, under the Davenport Brighton Bridge."

"Right," I said, my mind whirling.

"What do you want us to do, boss?"

"Get the guys ready to go to his meet. Two cars. Follow the usual routine. He's unbalanced, so make sure you're all wearing your bulletproof vests and keep your tempers. The last thing we want to do is start a war. There will be no winners."

"Will he kill her?"

"No, the greater problem is, he scares her enough that she starts to sing."

FOUR HOURS LATER, I was on the phone with Maxim as we slowly pulled up to the deserted base of the bridge. I spotted his black van. It was surrounded by his thugs, all dressed in his trademark black formal attire as if they were bouncers in a nightclub.

"I just arrived," I said to Maxim. "He has an army of his men around."

"Be careful," he warned. I could hear the worry in his voice.

He'd wanted to fly down immediately, but I told him I wanted to handle it myself. This was my problem.

"Yeah. Call you after I'm done with him," I said.

Just as I was about to end the call, he suddenly asked, "Push comes to shove, are you willing to give up the girl?"

"No," I snapped abruptly and ended the call.

The fact that he actually thought the question was warranted had set off a ball of suffocating fury into the pit of my stomach. The choice was coming down to either her or our entire conglomerate of operations in the country, and I already knew my choice.

And it seemed Bogdan had also made his choice. He must really want Bianca ... even at the price of his life.

I slipped my dark glasses on.

Sergei pulled the car door open for me and I stepped out as I straightened my cuffs.

Bogdan stepped out from his blacked-out SUV, his laughter boisterous and grating. He'd always been a burly man, a ferocious boxer in his younger days. Well, that was the past. Now, he was potbellied while decked out in thick extravagant gold chains and rings compliments of the empire he had built from people and Fentanyl trafficking.

He looked like such a parody of a low-class pimp from the eighties that I could hardly believe he had found the guts to do what he had.

"Our prince," he greeted sarcastically, his hands rising up in the air as he bowed mockingly as low as his thick stomach would let him.

Still, I noticed he had stopped a safe distance away from me. It told me he was nervous.

He knew he was playing with the big boys. He had grasped the tiger's tail and now, his hand was stuck on it and he had no choice but to face his fate. "Gracing us with your magnificent presence is a true privilege," he said.

I didn't react to his ridiculous drama. "You took Sarah Dale. You do know what that means don't you?" I asked calmly. "You just declared war on us ... and the US government."

The amusement drained from his face.

It would have been funny if Bianca weren't involved.

"I declare no war on no one!" he blurted out aggressively. "I'm just asking for what belongs to me. For what you have taken from me."

I took a deep breath and then released it. Slowly. Deliberately. "Where's Sarah?"

The corners of his lips lifted in a smug smile. He kept his gaze on me as he beckoned with a big meaty hand to his men.

A few seconds later, a woman greying at the temples was roughly dragged out of the van. Her hands were tied, there was duct tape across her mouth, and her face showed bruises.

I cursed inwardly.

She was the former acting Attorney General and now, Solicitor General of the state of New York.

Once again, I couldn't believe Bogdan's audacity. What did he think was going to happen to him once he set her free? Or if he actually killed her. He was as mad as a hatter.

Her eyes filled with terror as she looked wildly from Bogdan to me. She began to struggle and wave her head desperately as his men started to manhandle her.

"Let her go," I ordered.

Everyone went still. Even her. His men looked between their boss and me.

When he waved his hand, they let her go.

I immediately walked over to the woman and tore off the tape from across her lips.

"My Jacob" she cried, livid and frantic. "They have my Jacob."

"I know."

"Fix this or I'll destroy every one of you. Every single one of you," she threatened, some of the indomitable spirit that had made her rise to the top of her profession coming back to life.

"If you want to see him again, stay calm and do as you are told," I said, and turned to Bogdan.

At the look in my eyes, he backed away a few steps. He was afraid of me, but there was an odd smile playing on his lips. I realized then all my plans were shot to pieces. I couldn't predict what his next move would be, because he didn't behave like a normal man would. He belonged in a mental hospital for the criminally insane.

"Don't let him leave," Sarah begged, grabbing my forearm. "He's still got Jacob."

"Take her," Bogdan said to one of his men.

"You're not going to let them take me again?" she pleaded with me, her eyes wild.

"He will keep Jacob, but he will let you go. Just go back out there and behave normally. I will free Jacob. That is my promise to you," I told her.

"Remember you promised," she said bitterly.

"I promised," I confirmed.

Bogdan began to laugh. He made a motion towards his men, and one of the bouncer goons came forward.

Looking at me with pleading, fearful eyes, Sarah reluctantly went with him.

Both she and I knew Bogdan would set her free as she was only taken to make a statement. I turned towards Bogdan. "Where's her grandson?"

His smile was blinding. "Clean up your house," he said to me. "And if you happen to see what clearly doesn't belong to you, then send it back and I'll do the same ..." He paused to see my reaction.

I remained expressionless.

"If you fail to comply, dear Prince, I will ensure that she

sings, loud and clear about your family and your precious business. All your dirty dealings, the bribes she's collected, and the bodies she's buried for you. It will all start to stink like the shit that men pass when they are tortured to death and I will make sure that the world smells it."

"You want to take things this far, Bogdan?"

"You're the one who crossed the line!" he roared. "What gives you the right to interfere in my affairs? I keep trying to crack my skull on what your problem could possibly be, but I cannot think why the great Prince wants my woman. What do you want with my woman?"

I remained silent.

My silence enraged him. "You don't know what pain is do you? Embarrassment? Loss?" He wagged his fat forefinger at me. "Well, just sit and watch, *little Prince*, and see just what I, Bogdan, will do. What I will drive the Solicitor General of the state of New York to do. She wants her grandson back. Yes, yes, I will give him back to her. I will return him to her piece by piece. You have three days to return the woman and pay suitable compensation for all the damage you have caused to me and my business, or else I will bury your family ... and hers."

I turned around and returned to my waiting vehicle.

10

BIANCA

I paced the living room floor anxiously while waiting for Levan to come back. Outside, it was pouring with rain and crawling with heavily armed men dressed like they were part of a SWAT team. It literally felt as if I was in a war zone.

I stopped in front of a striking painting of a barely-clothed, crowned Poseidon in all his fleshy glory, riding a chariot of fierce white horses over a raging sea. He was surrounded by baby cupids who wore worried expressions on their cherubic little faces. In a way, it was the perfect imagery of the turbulent mess Levan and I were in.

The front door opened.

I scurried for a peep down the hallway.

Two of his men walked in.

I quickly retreated my head back until I heard another set of footsteps. I popped my head back around the door.

Levan stood there while shaking off droplets of rain from his jacket.

One of his men went forward and disappeared down the hallway to the side while Levan spoke to the other in words I could not hear.

I waited.

Soon enough, the one who'd disappeared, reappeared with an umbrella in hand. He spoke rapidly in Russian to his boss and then they all took their leave.

Levan came forward and stood in front of me. No smile showed on his face.

"What's going on?" I whispered.

"Do you want something to drink?" he asked

"Ok ..." I nodded, even though the last thing on my mind was food or drink.

"Come with me," he said and led the way in towards the kitchen.

I realized he hadn't touched me since he came in. It made my stomach twist with nervous fright, but then I reckoned if anything truly bad had happened, he wouldn't look so calm.

The kitchen was only lit by the frosted glass lamps on the wall and he didn't bother turning on any of the overhead lights. He went over to the electric kettle in the corner. It was already filled with water, so he switched it on, then turned around to face me.

I waited nervously by the door.

"Tea or coffee" he asked.

I heard him but my mind remained blank.

His dampened hair had been slicked away from his face, and in the cozy illumination of the room, he suddenly seemed to ooze a kind of primitive sexuality. If Aldie had been there, she would have described him as hot. But calling him hot would be like calling a panther a cat.

He was devastatingly magnetic. In the mood he was in, he promised of addictive, *raw* sex.

My eyes traveled down his body as I noted the way the material clung to the ridges of his torso, his triceps, and the bronzed skin of his veined arms exposed by the folded sleeves of his shirt. When my gaze moved lower to the way his pants fit to his lean hips and powerful thighs, something inside me felt as if it was melting and I became breathless. Which was totally crazy because of the dangerous situation I was in. Or maybe it was the thought of how easily it could have all come to an end for me that had made me become this unfamiliar, sex-crazed maniac.

"Bianca" he called.

My ogling ceased abruptly and suddenly, I became aware of the sound of the water boiling and the pitter-patter of the rain against the windows filling the tense silence between us. I dragged my eyes from the bulge in his pants, back to his face. "Uh ... what did you say?"

"Tea or coffee?" he repeated softly.

I frowned. "Uh ... you don't drink coffee at night. Oolong will be fine," I said it without thinking, but only when the corners of his mouth lifted in a tiny smile did I realize I had betrayed just how much I remembered of the past and him.

"And Earl Grey for you," he murmured softly.

A kind of wild happiness flooded my veins and all I wanted to do was throw myself at him and let the world outside be damned. My life had been one of sacrifice. Shoes that pinched, secondhand clothes that made the bullies at school sneer at me. From a very young age, I'd learned to go without to make my mother happy. Have you had enough food, she'd ask me, and I would nod, even though I was still hungry.

On the rare occasion I was invited to someone's birthday party I would save my slice of cake to share with my mother. I always saved the good half, the edge with the most icing and the cherry on it.

It broke my heart and I cried myself to sleep for days, but I even gave up Toto, the little stray dog that had followed me home from school one day, when we couldn't afford to feed him anymore. I can still see the look in his eyes when my mother and I dropped him off at the shelter.

I did it all without resentment because I loved her that much, but after she died, I found the habit of putting myself last had become ingrained in me. It was still almost impossible to push myself forward and take what I wanted. Even now.

I walked towards the island counter. "Any news?" I asked. "About my father?"

"Nothing yet," he said as he retrieved two boxes of tea bags from the cabinet above. "We're still trying to look for him and by all indications, he hasn't left the state. Do you have any ideas as to where he might have gone?"

I thought hard, but there was nothing in my head. My father's movements when he was not in my line of sight, had always been a mystery to me.

Levan set the two mugs of steaming hot tea before me.

I looked up into his eyes, and to my confusion, they seemed veiled and hard.

The man who had kissed me so passionately, who'd radiated such warmth and emotion in the boutique was nowhere to be found.

"Bogdan hasn't contacted you? You said that he'd figured out that you took me and then we rushed from the boutique. Surely, he must have contacted you by now."

"He hasn't," he said, and immediately turned away, taking his mug with him.

Something twisted in my stomach. I ran after him and stood in his way. "You're lying," I accused. His eyebrows dipped in annoyance, but I was never one to run away from my troubles. "Please don't lie to me, Levan. Tell me what's going on. Bogdan has contacted you, hasn't he?"

He watched me and it was like being transported in time. We were back in college. His gaze always so guarded but enchanting enough to have me hanging onto every word that came out of his mouth, each one sweet like honey. But our abrupt separation and the mountain of lies by omission he'd fed me about his identity, rang like a bell in my brain.

"We're still searching for your father. The most likely scenario is he has gone into hiding to protect himself." His eyes softened a fraction. "Don't worry about him. Self-preservation is always strong in men like your father. They are the ones who will survive a nuclear holocaust."

I felt some measure of relief, but I still felt completely in the dark. "What did Bogdan say?"

"The rules of my world are: the less you know the safer you will be. Will you trust me and let me solve this situation in my own way?"

I nodded slowly.

"Goodnight, Bianca," he said with a gentle smile. He stepped to the side and walked out of the kitchen.

I was too wound up to speak. I felt lost and bereft. I thought of what he said about my father and I knew instinctively that he was right. My father was a survivor. Pulling out my phone, I decided to check up on Aldie for the fiftieth time that day.

She however, did not pick up.

It was close to midnight so it was perfectly reasonable that she could be asleep, but Aldie had the supersonic ears of a bat ... her phone was never far away from her and it didn't seem possible that she would have not been awakened by my call. I dialed her number again, my steps quickening in haste as I reached the top of the stairs.

Still no response.

In a panic, I pounded on the heavy mahogany door of Levan's room. "Levan!" I shouted.

A few seconds later, he pulled it open. He wore nothing but the pants of the suit he'd worn earlier.

"Aldie," I blurted out, shoving the phone in his face. "She's not answering her phone."

"She's probably asle—"

"Aldie is an extremely light sleeper," I cried desperately. "If she isn't answering her phone then ..." I couldn't even say the words.

He whirled on his heel and strode into his room.

My heart was thundering in my chest as I watched him.

He retrieved his phone from his bedside table and dialed, pressed it to his ear, then blasted off a low concise inquiry in Russian.

Then he went *silent.*

A full freaking minute must have passed while he'd said neither a word, nor turned to me.

Shaking with fear, I walked in and stood in front of him. My eyes found his. "Is she okay?" I asked, afraid to even breathe.

"She's not coming to the door," he muttered.

My heart dropped into my stomach. I stared at him in horror as he said his next words.

"Break in," he ordered into his phone.

I held his gaze, my chest heavy, and my breathing hard.

"She will be fine," he said to me.

I heard the words as though he had whispered them into my ear, but they brought me no comfort. *Not Aldie. Not sweet Aldie.* She had done nothing to deserve this. "Not her," I whispered brokenly.

Levan put his hand around me.

I went willingly into his arms. In his arms, I felt peace and warmth emanating from his skin, soothing me in a way that made it easier for me to breathe.

"She'll be okay. I promise you. Bogdan doesn't want her," he murmured in my ear.

I focused on fighting off the tears gathering in my eyes.

A few minutes passed in his arms. I couldn't move. I couldn't think. The horror was too much to bear. *What if Bogdan had her? Oh, God!*

Then his cell rang.

I jumped like a startled cat.

He placed his cell phone against his ear.

The seconds ticked away as I watched wide-eyed. I inched closer to him and squeezed his forearm so he would bring his gaze to mine. *"Is she alright?"* I mouthed, but before he could answer me, my new phone rang in my hand.

It was Aldie.

"Aldie," I called urgently.

"What is it?" she asked, her voice just as panicked as mine.

"Where are you?"

"At home. I was asleep."

"But I was calling your phone," I insisted, confused.

"I put it on charge, but the charger wasn't plugged in properly. Are you okay? Is everything alright?"

"Aldie ..." I shut my eyes with relief. "Please ... be a bit more careful. This is a very dangerous time for us, and I don't—I wouldn't be able to live with myself if something happened to you because of me. Please, please make sure that I can reach you."

"I know, Bee ... I'm sorry." Her voice was quiet and full of remorse. "Work today was a nightmare, so I just collapsed into bed."

"Okay. It's okay. It's all good now," I said more to myself than her.

"Uh ... the men in my house? Just to be sure they're Levan's guys, right?"

I met Levan's gaze on me, dark and hooded. I quickly turned away, my nerves frayed and my composure shot to hell. "Uh, yeah."

"They broke my lock," she said. "I nearly died in my sleep from the bang. When will this be over, Bianca?"

"I don't know. Just please keep your phone on, Aldie, and be reachable at all times. And don't worry they'll fix your door. I'll call you in the morning, okay?"

"Okay, goodnight."

"And Aldie ... I love you."

"I love you too, Bee."

I ended the call and took a few seconds to compose myself then turned to him with the best smile I could muster, my heart full of relief and gratitude. "She's fine, thank you."

The way he looked at me ... made my heart almost stop. He raised his hand and all I could do was watch it with fascination as I waited with anticipation for the delicious tingle of his touch.

He placed his hand on my hair ... gently brushed it out of my face and tucked it behind my ear. "I want you to know this. Bogdan will never have you," he said his voice seeming to vibrate through my body. It felt like he was making an oath to me. His finger caressed my chin.

My skin felt warm at the contact. I shuddered, jittery, sweaty and completely out of my mind. He could have done anything with me at that moment.

He ran his finger along my lower lip. Then he closed his eyes and swallowed. When he opened them again, he took a step back and smiled at me. "Go to sleep, Bianca. There is far, far more at stake than slaking my lust for you."

For a second, I stared at him. Then I turned and fled from his room.

11

S omehow, I finally found sleep in the early hours of the morning and was in a deep sleep when a wet tongue started lapping at my face. My eyelids snapped open to a pair of round brown eyes staring right back at me.

"*Biscuit*," I cried with a laugh, as the corgi puppy Aldie and we owned together, started yelping excitedly and jumping all over me. I let him do his usual thing and dive bomb my body, until I realized something. If the pup was here ... I grabbed him and shot up to a sitting position. "Aldie!" I called, when I saw her.

She stood in the doorway, a small suitcase in her hand, and a goofy grin on her face.

"What the ... how did *you* get here?" I asked.

"I come bearing clothes," she said.

It seemed Biscuit had no time for social niceties, especially not when there was a sea of overpriced sheets where he could go bat-shit crazy. He struggled so hard in my arms, I had to give in and fall back into a prone position. Laughing, I fought off his wet kisses valiantly, until I was eventually able to wriggle away enough to almost fall out of bed.

Aldie looked amused as she watched me try to catch my breath.

With my palm, I rubbed off the wet saliva residue he'd left on my skin. "How did you guys get here?"

"Levan sent his men for me," she answered. "He thought we might like to spend the day together and since our front door is busted, I thought ... why not?"

Snippets of the previous evening flashed into my head and I flushed.

Her eyes widened and she hurried over to me. "Did something happen between the two of you?"

My gut twisted in what felt like painful disappointment. "Nope, nothing did," I said, as I hurried away towards the bathroom with Biscuit following on his non-existent legs. If I thought that would end the conversation I was sorely wrong.

Aldie came after me, her face determined and curious. "Bianca? What happened?" she persisted.

I pulled out my toothbrush from the cabinet. "Did you see him on your way in?"

"Yeah," she answered, rightfully surprised. "He opened the door for me. With this house, one would assume that he has an army of servants ready to do his bidding."

"He does," I said. "They are very discreet. I have only met his housekeeper."

"Well, as we've found out so far, discretion is his strong suit, or perhaps the rule of his trade. You can't be one of the most notorious *Bratva* families in the country and afford to have any loose mouths around you." She chewed at her lip. "Strange, but he still seems to be the same extraordinarily handsome, kind, normal guy we knew, despite the new light on his identity."

"There's nothing *same* about him," I mumbled through the toothbrush in my mouth.

She wrinkled her nose at me in the mirror. "I didn't catch that," she said. "Same or sane?"

I didn't bother clarifying.

She chuckled. "Are you still pissed at him?"

I spat into the sink. "No. My heart says, why didn't he damn well contact me when he got better, but my head says, how can I be mad at him? He showed me his wounds and if not for him, I would be doing God only knows what kind of degrading thing with Bogdan by now. Bogdan already warned me in no uncertain terms that those things would repulse me, but I would have to obey him at all times." I couldn't help the shudder that ran through me. Even the thought of touching him made me feel dirty. I started to take off my clothes to get into the shower.

Aldie pulled a disgusted expression. "That sounds like a fate worse than death. Let's not talk about that now. Levan has offered to help make breakfast. What do you want?"

I opened the shower cubicle door. "I think we should minimize how much we take from him, don't you?"

She waved her hand dismissively and turned to take her leave. "Nonsense," she said in a totally fake English accent. "You'll eat whatever we make. C'mon, Biscuit."

"Aldie, I think that's enough."

"The recipe says two cups."

"That's three," I pointed out.

"Two, three, what's the difference?" she asked airily.

"Not everyone likes it that sweet," I found myself saying.

Her head whirled around towards me. Her eyes were shining and there was a *gotcha* expression on her face. "Hmmm ... what about dried berries? Are we going to add some of those in?"

Bianca loved smooth pancakes, but at the risk of exposing myself even further, I let it go. "Sure, why not?" I said with a shrug and stepped away from the kitchen counter.

She laughed uproariously. "You wanted to make her breakfast this morning and used me as a cover, didn't you? Wow, I can't believe I had to be shipped all the way from a different island to help your romantic agenda."

I wished it were as she described it. That Bogdan and his men didn't exist. That I had simply brought her here for a fun breakfast. The idea was so filled with innocence and so alluring, I wanted to hold on to it.

"I should be offended," she went on, wagging her finger at me. "That you never revealed yourself as an Ivankov, but fortunately for you, I like playing Cupid and I love Bianca, so I want something amazing for her. And you might be that amazing person. Get the butter out for me, can ya?"

Meekly, I went to the refrigerator and pulled out a tub of butter.

"The thing about Bianca is she has no confidence in herself. It's like it's been set in stone inside her that the best is not destined for her. She doesn't deserve it. Sometimes, I even think she doesn't know how to reach out and grab for what she wants. And the one time she did it with you, you disappeared, and that really set her back. But the truth is you're still sweet on her, aren't you?"

I frowned as I put the pan on the stove. "We're friends, Aldie."

She laughed. "Friends don't do what you did for her. You risked everything to steal Bianca away from Bogdan. You may be able to gloss over the fact that what you did was the nuclear option with Bianca, but not with me. My grandmother is Russian, remember? And Bridgeport is a small place. I've heard whispers and horror stories about Bogdan from the time I was ten years old. Selling his Fentanyl to our kids, taking Russian women for his brothels, and we knew to stay clear from him and his businesses. But now the whole community is in an uproar and there's all kinds of gossip flying around about him."

I put the pan on the fire and turned to her casually. "What kind of gossip?"

She stopped stirring the batter. "That he's the one who's taken the Solicitor General and her grandson. That he's using her to blackmail you."

My expression didn't change.

Still, her eyes widened. "Wow, so it's true! He did take the Solicitor General." She shook her head in amazement. "Do you know he's turned Bridgeport upside down with the buzz for us to prepare for all-out war? For the first time, someone is going all gangbusters to take your family out. He's promised the pavements will be lined with dead bodies and the streets will become rivers of blood if anyone gets involved and helps you."

I understood the instill fear technique and why he was utilizing it, but the way he was involving the community outside our world, made my hands clench. It had been unhinged psychopaths spraying indiscriminate violence into society in general that eventually caused the Italian Mafia's demise.

Ultimately though, I had to take the blame for the way the situation had played out. When I took Bianca, I didn't have a plan. I just reacted from the gut and on the assumption that

Bianca was just another woman to him. He was well known for treating his women like they were nothing to him, sharing and gifting them around like they were boxes of cheap candy. I myself, once saw him at a party offer the woman he was with to someone he was trying to do business with. But I never thought he would start a war over one.

"Regardless how this all ends," Aldie went on, "he's just opened up a can of worms, hasn't he? It was only a rumor before that that the Solicitor General was in your pocket, but now it's pretty much confirmed. I'm right, aren't I?"

I didn't say anything.

"The only way out now, is if you save the Solicitor General and kill Bogdan."

I cut a bit of butter, threw it into the pan, and watched it sizzle. Pancakes were the only thing I could cook.

"You're going to save her, right?" There was no mistaking the fear and concern in her tone.

I faced her and held out my hand for the bowl of batter. "You know I can't say anything to you."

She expelled the breath she was holding and put the bowl into my outstretched hand. "I know, but throw me a crumb, won't you?"

"We're more powerful than you think," I said softly.

"How big is the pile of bodies going to be for this to come to an end?" she whispered.

I wondered the same. I carefully ladled batter into the pan. "I won't let anything happen to either of you."

"And what about you?" she asked. "Bullets know no names. And according to Bianca, you already have four writing up a story on your chest."

I was about to answer her when all the hairs on my body rose to attention. Bianca was around. I glanced towards the doorway, and saw her watching us with large haunted eyes.

She wore a white t-shirt with a faded cupcake on it, tucked into a pair of grey shorts. She held the puppy in her arms.

Aldie's head whirled around in the direction I stared at. "Hey you," she greeted with a bright smile.

My eyes on the first batch of batter I had poured into the pan, I waited for Bianca's response but when she didn't immediately say anything, I knew she must have heard part of our conversation. I lifted my eyes from the pancake.

"Solicitor General? What heap of bodies?" she asked, putting the dog on the ground.

Aldie made a weird sound. One, I'm sure was meant to brush over Bianca's concerns, but it only made her sound as guilty as hell. I flipped the pancake. It was perfectly golden brown.

"Is someone going to tell me what's going on?" Bianca demanded.

"Nothing is going on," Aldie answered. "We were just chatting." With a smile, she looked away.

Bianca's angry gaze moved to me.

I met it head on, but she took my breath away. A painful jolt of awareness shot straight to my groin. Somehow, being furious made her look even more beautiful. Her disapproving gaze burned me in all the right places and it was as insane as it was exhilarating.

"I'm guessing you're not going to answer me either." She headed over to the counter to pull out a stool and plop herself on it. "Since both of you seem to connect with each other more than I ever will with either of you, then maybe, you should take advantage of your Russian comradery and actually speak the damn language. If you're going to keep me in the dark, the least you could do is to freaking do it properly."

She was pissed and I didn't blame her, but the less she knew the better for her.

Aldie took the victim route. "Why would you be eavesdropping on our conversation?"

Bianca ignored her and poured herself some orange juice from the carton sitting on the counter.

My first pancake was done. I slid it expertly onto a plate, sprinkled some blueberries and cranberries on top, then took it to her.

She looked up at my arrival, her eyes were so bright in the morning light they completely stopped me in my tracks.

"What?" she asked.

I wondered if she realized I would do anything for her. I was so thoroughly and completely in her grasp that it made my chest constrict with fear. Breaking her gaze, I laid the plate in front of her.

Before I could walk away, she grabbed my hand.

Aldie, seemingly oblivious to the strong currents in the room, was cutting up more strawberries.

My heart was thumping in my chest.

Bianca rose to her feet and stood in front of me. Her head barely reached my shoulders. Her hair was piled on top of her head with strands framing her beautiful face. "Levan," she pleaded. "Please tell me what's going on."

Somehow, I found a smile. "Wouldn't Aldie be easier to coax?"

She shot a look at her best friend.

"Impossible," Aldie called out. "She knows I'm immune to her antics."

"And I'm not?" I asked my brows rising.

"Only one way to find out," Aldie replied, her eyes filling with amusement. She bit into a strawberry and leaned against the counter to watch the show.

I returned my gaze to Bianca, but before my eyes could even connect with hers she had lifted herself to the tips of her toes and pressed her lips to mine.

All reason was instantly blasted out of me.

My mouth was filled with the taste that drove me wild and at the same time left me spineless. There wasn't a better feeling in the world. "Bianca," I muttered as I tried to pull my lips away from her.

Undeterred, she linked her hands around my neck, and slipped her tongue into my mouth. She drank in my flavor, her tongue dancing against mine ... then just as suddenly as she began, she broke it off. With her fingers to her lips as if she could not believe what she had just done, she took a step backwards.

I remained stunned into immobilization.

"Fucking hell," Aldie muttered.

Bianca took another step backwards. She opened her mouth to speak but then shut it, her face tightening. She turned around to leave.

I grabbed her by her t-shirt and without a word, I turned her around, pulling her with me despite her protests.

"Aldie," she cried.

Her best friend, who seemed to be beside herself with amusement, had turned Judas though. "Take her away, Levan" she called treacherously. "Don't bring her back until you're both good and ready."

"Levan ..." Bianca struggled, breathlessly.

I didn't let go until we were in the office down the hall. I pulled her inside and shut the door behind me,

Before I could speak, she did, "I didn't mean that," she said.

I scowled at her.

"Aldie ... she pushed me to it." She held her hands up in surrender or apology. "That was just me being absolutely stupid. I'm so sorry. I shouldn't have done that."

"Okay." There wasn't a trace of amusement in my tone. With a hard look at her, I turned and left the room.

13

BIANCA

"What did he do?" Aldie asked the moment I returned.

I took a seat and stabbed my pancake with a fork. I hated myself right now. I had never behaved so irresponsibly or so crazily in my life before.

She hurried over to me, spatula in hand. "Well?"

"Let it go, Aldie. Let's just try to find my dad and bring this whole thing to an end."

"There's nothing we can do about finding him. When your dad wants to disappear for good, he does."

I tore off a tiny piece of the pancake and held it out to Biscuit. "You're right," I said. "The only time he was really present and in contact at all times was when we all knew Mom wasn't going to make it. Before that, he would be gone for weeks at a time without either of us knowing where he was."

"Exactly," she said, rubbing my arm in consolation.

"He cares," I said, even though the statement tasted like bile in my mouth. "He does. He is a complete mess, but when he figured out Mom was dying, he rushed back and he never left until the last day."

Aldie squeezed my hand.

"Do you think that perhaps he is not aware of what has happened?" I asked hopefully.

"Well, he's usually great at watching from afar," Aldie said dryly.

"Not when it's this serious," I said, trying to convince myself more than her. "Not when our lives are on the line."

She had bent down to pick up Biscuit, but I didn't miss the look she tried to hide.

"What?" I asked.

"Nothing."

"Aldie ..."

She sighed. "Don't take this the wrong way but this time, it's a little bit different."

"How so?"

"His life is on the line too. I'm not trying to shit on your dad, but he's not exactly been the model father. He framed it well with all his talk of downing sleeping pills and a bottle of vodka, but at the end of the day, he *did* sell you off to Bogdan to save his own sorry skin."

I opened my mouth to answer her.

She showed me her palm and carried on talking, "Even back then, when he came back to stay it was not because he was being loyal and good. Your mom had insurance, so he didn't have to shell out anything, and ... she had the bakery. It might not be much, but he did then and does even now, raid the cash register a couple of times a month, doesn't he?"

Something hard and painful struck my heart at her words. Of course, she was right, but all my life, I had been denied my father's love and yearned for it. So, I had simply learned to make excuses for him. I wasn't a child anymore. I could see the truth as clear as day. My father didn't love me. He only came to raid my cash register and steal a few chocolate chip cookies from the counter. Like a fool, I would pack them for him to take away. God, I was so stupid. "Perhaps he does know," I said, my voice sounding flat, my heart filled with grief for the man I'd always loved, but had absolutely no confidence in. "Perhaps he doesn't care. Perhaps, he is looking only to save himself and is keeping himself hidden until all of this blows over."

She must have felt bad for me, because she shrugged and her tone was kind as she spoke, "Or perhaps not. Maybe he does love you in his own way. Let's just focus on ending this situation with Bogdan. We'll see how things turn out with your dad then. To be honest, I hope he remains hidden. He could just mess it up if he shows up now by giving Bogdan another bargaining chip. I have complete trust in Levan and I know he can solve this. Somehow."

"I've just told the only man that could help me to fuck off," I cried.

Her head jerked back. "You didn't say that."

"Well, not in obvious terms, but ..."

She sighed then and put the puppy down. "What's your issue with Levan? Why don't you want to let him in? You're still pissed tha—"

"He's a criminal, Aldie. Don't you remember my list?"

"What list?"

"The list of professions I never want to date," I reminded her.

"Ah, soldiers, pilots, policemen ..."

"... And firefighters," I completed for her.

"Criminal isn't on there?"

"Serial killers aren't either, but maybe I should grant them leniency too."

"Slow down viper ... I was just saying."

I sighed. "I don't want to fall in love with someone who'll just die suddenly. Levan already nearly died."

"But you're already at least half in love with him, all over again."

"No, I'm not."

"Oh yeah?"

"I know what happens when you fall in love with the wrong guy. Mom fell in love with my dad, a street thug who promised her the world, and it all went downhill from there."

"Levan isn't the same as your dad," she said quietly.

"No, he isn't," I agreed. "He's the Russian equivalent with a whole lot more power and money which makes him a thousand times more lethal to me. I'll go to sleep every night wondering if by the time I wake up, my lover and my soulmate will be dead. My dream is a peaceful life."

There was a ding then and both of our gazes lifted to the oven.

"I'm heating some frozen pizza," she said smacking her hands together.

"I thought we were having pancakes?"

"You're having pancakes. I'm having pizza." She squealed with excitement. "And I also found some really freaking expensive Beluga caviar so I'm making some Caviar Blini too. I plan to sneak those home with me."

I shook my head at her. "You're stealing caviar now?"

"Relax. He has so much in his fridge and he told me to help myself to anything I want." She looked down at me haughtily. "You're not the only one with a relationship with Master Ivankov." She reverted to her fake English accent. "If anything, my relationship with him is more defined and slightly older than yours."

I rolled my eyes at her as she went to the oven to get her pizza.

Biscuit, a greedy little bugger, scurried after her.

She opened the oven door and the delicious yeasty, cheesy smell of pizza wafted over. She pulled it out, put it on the counter, and cut it into slices.

I turned away in thought, a crazy idea stirring in my mind, but it was a scary thought. A very scary thought. A thought that involved rejection. "What if I asked him?" I blurted out.

Aldie walked towards me, carrying the pizza. "Ask him what?"

I couldn't bring myself to speak out loud, so I gazed at her, hoping she would understand without me having to speak.

"Ask him what?" she asked sitting down and pulling out a slice.

I suddenly lost my courage. "Forget it," I said, rising restlessly to my feet.

She got it then and her mouth widened into a massive *oh.* "It's not like he has an ordinary business, Bianca. I don't think he can just ... leave?"

There, she said it ... I had my answer. "Okay, forget I said anything."

14

LEVAN

https://www.youtube.com/watch?v=otAu5twqDpk

I finished my call with Sarah, who had ranted and raved at me for ten minutes straight, as I threw my phone on my desk. I couldn't blame her. She wanted her grandson back. Rubbing the back of my neck, I watched Bianca through the window of my study.

It was late and Aldie had already been taken to a safe house where she would mostly remain until this mess was over. If things went my way, hopefully, it would be over very soon.

I'd hoped bringing Aldie here would keep Bianca occupied and take her mind off her troubles for a little while, but it seemed as if things had become even more tense and strained between us since her visit.

She had retired to the poolside the moment Aldie went, her

headphones firmly glued to her ears, and her eyes closed. That was two hours ago.

For some reason, her dog had decided to stay with me. I guess, surreptitiously feeding a dog treats will make it do that. I looked down at him.

He blinked and wagged his tail encouragingly.

"Nothing is for free," I told him. "Eventually, you have to pay for everything."

He began to pant.

I dropped another little treat next to him.

He scoffed it down and looked up at me with begging eyes.

"Let's go. Time to earn your keep," I said as I turned away from the window. I had my hands in my pockets, giving the picture of a leisurely approach, but my heart was thumping in my chest. It never failed to surprise me just how undone I could become where Bianca was concerned.

As we got closer, the dog ran on ahead, taking a flying leap, landing on her. The impact almost threw her off the lounger.

Attaboy!

"Biscuit," she scolded, but I noticed she didn't try to push the dog away as he leaned forward and enthusiastically began to lick her face. When the dog settled on her lap, she reached for the phone that the dog's greeting had flung out of her grasp.

I was immediately on it. Our hands came within inches of

the other as I reached the device first. Our gazes met ... and she jerked back. I retrieved the phone and held it out to her.

"Thank you," she said, awkwardly yanking her earphone out of one of her ears, as she took the phone.

I didn't miss the way she ensured that we did not make physical contact.

Holding onto the dog as if for dear life, she chewed her bottom lip nervously and stared out at the grounds beyond the pool.

"Do you know how to swim?" I asked.

"Uh ... not really. I'm better at floating around." She finished her statement with a short laugh.

"What's amusing?"

"Me. It seems as though that's all I've been doing my whole life. Floating around aimlessly."

The dog wriggled out of her lap, and wandered away.

"It's the same way for a lot of us. In case, you haven't noticed," I said softly.

"I haven't noticed," she said bitterly. "Everyone else seems to have their feet solidly on the ground, their lives mapped out. They do what pleases them."

"You haven't been paying attention then."

She met my gaze, and this time around, held it. There was no bitterness, no anger, no blame in her eyes. The seconds ticked away and it almost seemed as though we had reached a sort of truce. Like in this moment, despite our differences, we could allow ourselves to be lost in the unspoken admiration we both held for the other.

It came to a startling end.

There was a heart twisting squeal, accompanied by a heavy plop and splash, as Biscuit fell into the water.

"Oh, my God!" she gasped shooting out of the lounger. "He can't swim, Levan!" she shouted as she ran to the steps leading into the pool.

The dog looked fine as it paddled happily in the water.

Not one to let a golden opportunity go to waste, I was already airborne, clothes and all. I dove in close to the animal and caught it, just before it became clear that he was actually having the time of his life. I held him solidly in my arms. He'd just earned every single treat he had gotten from me.

On her knees and with relief across her face Bianca waited for our arrival by the edge of the pool. "I'm so sorry, Levan," she apologized her arms open to receive her pup from me.

"No problem," I said suavely, handing him over to her.

She hugged the wet creature tightly to her body. "Oh you poor baby. Are you alright?" Then she tried to lift him up to her, but with the slippery ease of an eel, he wriggled out of her arms and landed on the tiled floor, where he began to ferociously shake the water off his body. Bianca squealed and tried to shield herself from the hail of droplets, but with another great shake, he calmly wandered away towards the house.

Smart guy, knew his job was done for the day.

She glanced at me as she rose to her feet. "I better go grab him. He's going to mess up the house."

"Help me out, first," I said before she could hurry off.

Without thinking, she reached for the hand I held out.

I grabbed it and pulled her into the water with me.

She shrieked with shock all the way into the water, then shot back up a moment later with a gasp. "Levan!" she shouted, kicking furiously to stay afloat. "What the hell? It's the fucking deep end."

I grabbed her by the waist.

"Damn you," she cursed, but to keep herself afloat, she held onto me tightly.

I pulled her against me until our bodies were glued together and so were our gazes.

She brushed her hair out of her face. "You're going to pay for this," she breathed unsteadily.

"You have to put a bit more rancor into that kind statement to make it work," I murmured. My eyes ran over her breathtakingly beautiful face, my hands were twitching with the need to undress her. I had always been careful around her, to ensure I kept myself in check against the train-wreck of lust I devolved into whenever I was near her.

But today, I was absolutely done with any kind of restraint. Today, I refused to hold myself back. For all I knew, this moment would never come again. I could be dead tomorrow.

I slanted my head and captured her lips. I was immediately engulfed; ruthlessly and by a pleasure so intense, it caused pain. She tried to pull away, but there was no escaping me. Her taste was like no other, the perfect ignition to my madness and my complete loss of control.

Her hands continued to push half-heartedly at my shoulder, while my mouth went on ravishing hers, sucking on her tongue as I drank her in hungrily. My insides felt as if they were being torched. If I did not have her ...

Then it happened.

15

---

https://www.youtube.com/watch?v=R2LQdh42neg

Her hands stopped pushing and snaked around my neck. Not breaking the contact, I moved us to the shallower part of the pool. Her back met the edge and her feet settled on the floor.

She whimpered helplessly into my mouth.

I tore my mouth away and stared deeply into her eyes. I wanted to see this moment. Just in case, I never got this chance again.

She was beyond beautiful. Her mouth red and swollen and her cheeks looking flushed. Her pupils were so dilated they were amazing to see. Her breathing was as ragged as mine.

"Tell me you don't want me." I dared her, or perhaps I needed her to stop me since I had completely lost control.

"Tell me you don't feel as consumed as I do." I pressed my nose to her neck and breathed her in. "I'm addicted to your scent ... your flavor ..." I traced wet, sensual kisses along her jaw, then lifted her right out of the water, so I could suck on a clothed breast.

She cried out, her grip on my shoulders tightening as her head fell back in wonder.

Underneath her clothes, I could feel how hard her nipple was. I brought her back to eye level. "Tell me you don't want me and I'll stop. Right this moment."

Her eyes misted over as her gaze locked with mine, searching. She opened her mouth to speak but no words came out. Eventually, she gave up on any attempt at speech, we both knew it would only be lies, and crushed her lips to mine. Her kiss was hard and desperate. We needed each other in a way that neither of us could fully understand yet, or was willing to acknowledge.

The rush of joy bursting through me in this moment was intense, so intense I felt light-headed. "Hold on tight," I rasped as she wrapped her legs around mine. Grabbing the edges of her blouse, I yanked it off her head. The sports bra underneath joined the blouse somewhere in the bottom of the pool. My hands covered her beautiful swollen mounds, her pink nipples, hardened and ready for my touch. I gazed at them, taking my fill of the part of her body I had imagined and yearned for more times than was possible to count.

I sucked hard on the beautiful buds, even grazing the erect peaks with my teeth.

She jumped at the touch. Breathlessly, she ground her hips

against my swollen cock, straining aggressively through my slacks. Her hands clawed at the material of my shirt as she attempted to release it from my belt. She succeeded. Her fingernails scratched my skin ... the sweetest pain I'd ever experienced.

I released the button of my trousers, and had barely torn the zipper down when she took over. She slid her hand in to grab my cock through my briefs and fisted me ... and my body became like a live electric wire.

She lifted her gaze to mine, her eyes sparkling with the reflection of the water.

I could only stare back, a dumb beast in her thrall.

"Yes, I fucking want you," she muttered, and leaned forward.

I'd never known her to have a dirty mouth, and this was a side of her I had waited way too long to see. She nibbled on my lower lip and licked it, the way feral, free animals did.

I couldn't breathe as I watched her. So this was how it was, when your feelings for someone went way beyond the physical attraction. I wanted to watch her, but at the same time, I couldn't wait to have her. She growled at me and I felt possessed. I moved, not even registering what I was doing until I found myself grabbing her by the thighs. Lifting her clean out of the water, I sat her on the tiles.

Unsmiling and just as hungrily, she stared back at me. Then she reached for the button of her shorts.

The sound of a zipper opening had never sounded so heavenly. I stared mesmerized as she pulled the material down. The world outside of us stopped existing. Only just us in this pool floated in the universe. She flung the shorts aside and was about to take that last tiny scrap of cloth off, when I stopped her.

In a strange trance, I placed her legs over my shoulders.

Her thighs shut closed in response, trapping me between her slice of heaven. There was nowhere else I wanted to be. Her scent tantalized me—no, it hypnotized me. I'd waited so long for this moment. Very gently, I pushed the tiny material apart and gazed at her sweet secret. She was shaved clean and inside her slit, pink wet flesh quivered. Dirty, dirty lust rumbled in the pit of my stomach. I reached under her ass to pull her cunt to me, and gave the slick flesh a long, slow, lick.

"Ahhh," she moaned.

Pure ecstasy radiated through me. I fucking loved how she tasted, sweet and pure, and it made me wonder if I would ever be satiated enough. As she writhed and moaned above me, I dug my tongue into her, lapping up her juices as they flowed out. Driving my tongue between her folds, I feasted on her peachy sweetness till she almost tore my hair from my scalp. Then, and only then, did I allow myself to suck on her swollen bud, the white tip protruding out.

"Holy fuck, Levan," she cried.

Then I felt her unravel for me. She started to pull away from me but I held her tightly and in moments, her orgasm began … a force to be reckoned with too. Like a tsunami, it destroyed her. As the torrents of deep ecstasy tore through her body, her eyes rolled up into her head, her mouth opened in a soundless scream. Her body became as hard as a board. I could actually hear her heart thudding loud and fast in her chest. I stared with sheer wonder at what her euphoria had done to her.

When it was all over, her eyes closed and she went limp.

Holding her up, I lapped at her juices, licking her clean. Then I pulled her back into the water with me. Her eyes opened and I found them almost hazy, like someone who was still in shock. It made me feel possessive and protective of her.

She was mine. Forever. No man would ever see her like this but me.

Suddenly, she drove her tongue into my mouth. She was no longer holding back, her arms around my neck and one hand clawed in my hair as she kissed me wildly. Her other hand found its way down my torso, past the light dusting of hair at my groin, and grabbed my cock, this time boldly and uninhibitedly. She whispered very clearly into my ears, "Fuck me, Levan. I can't wait another second to feel you inside me."

"Neither can I, baby," I replied, and tore that last scrap of white satin away.

"Very caveman," she quipped, in an attempt to inject some humor into a situation that seemed like it was spiraling out of control, but both of us knew, humor couldn't contain this. This was beyond anything either of us had known or felt, or even expected from the other. This was pure madness. A beautiful madness.

"Hold on to me," I said, and she threw her hands around my shoulders.

"You're fucking beautiful," I breathed the words out, as I made sure her legs were properly fitted around me.

I grabbed her ass and she circled the rim of her upper lip with her tongue in anticipation.

"Do that again," I ordered, entranced.

Staring into my eyes, she did it again.

"Fuck," I muttered as she grabbed my throbbing cock and guided it to her entrance. I shut my eyes, leaning my forehead against hers to savor my first joining with her. She was made for me, her pussy perfectly fitted and snug around my cock. I had no doubt now that I had come home. This was the woman I was created solely to fuck and it was clearer to me than nothing else ever had been.

I almost couldn't believe it. She had been the dream that got away for so long. All these long years I told myself, the sacrifice was necessary. It was a sign of how deeply I cared for her. Now, I knew. It was bullshit. We were meant to be together. Nothing was more important than us. I would give everything up for her.

She tightened her muscles and her sex closed around me, slick and greedy as fuck, and I stopped thinking and plunged into her. I lost my head then. For the first time in my life, I felt my throat constrict with the need to cry like a baby. Tears filled my eyes as I licked the pulse ticking furiously in her neck.

I would never take all this beauty for granted.

Then I began to trace kisses along her jaw as I moved in and out of her in a gentle rhythm, relishing every moment as fire blazed through my veins. I couldn't even remember my own name but I thought of hers, over and over again, as though it were a prayer. The water lapped peacefully around us. It was truly beautiful. If I died tomorrow, it would be okay.

"Thank you," I muttered almost incoherently while she whimpered against me. I knew her nails were clawing into my back, but I registered nothing.

"Levan," she sang out my name as I increased my tempo and tunneled into her, again and again. Our harsh ragged breathing was loud in the quiet night as our bodies thrashed against each other.

"Ahhh ..." she moaned, long and tortuously.

I drove even harder and faster into her.

"Oh, my God, Oh Lev ... oh, fuuuuck."

I pounded into her until I felt her begin to tense with her impending release. I had long been consumed with the desperate need to come, but I was determined to wait until she was ready.

Her sex tightened around me, clenching so hard, the reins of my tenuous control finally slipped from my grasp. I couldn't hold on any longer then. I exploded inside her, just as she found her release, screaming out loud into the night as I buried my face in her neck and dropped over the edge into the beautiful abyss of sheer pleasure.

"Oh God," she said, quivering violently against me and bit hard into my shoulder to muffle herself.

I savored even that pain.

A long groan tore out of me as I drew near to the end of my climax. The very life had been drained out of my bones at the orgasm she had just given to me, but I couldn't let her go, or pull myself out of her.

Until death do us part, Bianca.

Until death do us part.

16

BIANCA

https://www.youtube.com/watch?v=jZIoxwoca9E

I awoke naked in Levan's bed. I was almost scared to open my eyes, nervous at the reality that life would bring me when I did. I opened my eyes and found myself alone in the vast bed. I could hear the sound of water running in the shower so I knew I would be safe for at least a few minutes. I rolled over, buried my face in the indentation left by Levan's head on his pillow, and breathed in deeply. First, I smelled his shampoo, then underneath it, his intoxicating scent.

In the past, I'd heard my friends say how a guy had screwed their brains out, and I had always inwardly raised an eyebrow to ridiculous and far-fetched statements like that. As if sex could be that good ...

It certainly had *never* been like that for me. From my first time in the back of Lincoln Wilson's father's sky blue Buick.

We were in high school and he was a senior. All the girls wanted Lincoln. During summer break, he would drive all the way down from Connecticut every weekend to take me out on dates.

This courtesy, which I'd deemed meant he must truly care, had led me down the path of an anti-climatic night that I wished had never happened. Not only was the sex awkward and painful, it permanently freed Lincoln from the desire to make the journey down from Connecticut to see me. And the three other encounters since then deserved to be forgotten. They were that unremarkable and limp.

But Levan.

Oh, my God, Levan.

He *screwed my brains out*! All freaking night long. In positions I didn't even know it was possible to get into.

It actually felt as if my brains had dropped somewhere on the floor. My head felt light and strange. I rolled my shoulders in circular movements, my whole body still felt hot and flushed with the after waves of unbelievable pleasure.

And my heart ... it wanted to burst.

I couldn't believe how much I had allowed him to do to me last night. He had had his head between my legs and his mouth on my sex. No man had ever even wanted to do that to me. Especially not the way he had done. He had eaten me out as if he was starving for me. His tongue had dug inside of me as deep as it would go.

Oh, God!

We didn't use a condom. I frowned at the memory. The other bad news was I had absolutely no recollection of saying goodnight or how I had got under the duvet. The moment he'd made me come for the fifth or sixth time, I must either have fallen asleep or passed out. The latter was scarier.

I heard the shower stop ... I quickly dove back onto my side of the bed and pulled the duvet up to my shoulders.

For some weird reason the impending confrontation with him made me nervous. What if like Lincoln, he had permanently lost the desire for more sex with me. While I couldn't believe how much I wanted to do it again. Actually, *right now*.

My stomach burned with heat and my breath shortened at the sudden ache between my thighs.

The door to the room opened and instead of behaving like a sophisticated woman who was sexily waking up to her lover, I squeezed my eyes shut like an idiot and stopped breathing. I heard his footsteps approach. There was still time to open my eyes and stop being a fool, but my eyelids wouldn't work.

He stopped at the bed. "I know you're awake, Bianca," he murmured.

Damnit, there was amusement in his voice.

"You're awfully still. Wave your hand or something if you want me to leave without a word, so that you can run out without having to face me."

I still didn't move. Shit. How did I get out of this one gracefully?

"Okay then, I guess you want me to leave," he said.

I shook my head so hard he burst into laughter, and I hated him for it.

I opened my eyes and my mouth went dry. A small towel was draped around his lean hips, water droplets still clung to his body, and his eyes were full of desire. He wanted me. He still wanted me.

He reached out a hand and grasping the edge of the duvet, he yanked it off me. His Adam's apple moved as he swallowed hard at the sight of me on the bed. "You're a sight for sore eyes, baby," he whispered hoarsely. His large hands closed around my thighs. For a second he did nothing, then he opened them wide. "Jesus, look how swollen you are," he breathed and leaning forward, he swiped his hot, eager tongue all the way up my slit.

I gasped with shock and pleasure when he speared me with it. He got on the bed and using his tongue as a piston he tongue-fucked me. Just when I thought I would die with all the delicious sensations flooding my body, he sucked my whole pussy into his mouth.

I was so sensitive from everything he had done to me last night, I nearly screamed. My body arched and my fingers were rakes in his silky hair. He slowed down then, and began to gently suck and eat me out. It was a glorious feeling. When my climax came, there was no way I could stop the scream that came from deep inside me. I shook and trembled as he held on and continued to lap on my juices.

Finally, when he had licked me completely clean, he stood.

I could see he had a massive hard-on, but to my surprise, he didn't want to act on it.

He pulled at the duvet that slightly covered me, and said, "Come and join me for breakfast when you're ready. I have some questions to ask you about your father." Then he went to the next room, which must be his dressing room.

I heard him move around for a few minutes, the sound of a door closing, then silence. He was gone. I stretched my sore limbs before throwing the luxurious comforter off me and rising.

I jumped out of bed, wrapped myself in a dressing gown draped across a leather lounge chair and scuttled off to my own room.

A few minutes later, I was in the shower and surprised at myself. I hadn't wanted to wash him off me. As the hot water cascaded down on me, my soapy hands had slipped between my thighs. My sex was so swollen it protruded out of me. Still, I wanted his mouth on me and his thick cock inside me again. In the full-length mirror, I stared at my reflection curiously.

Something had changed. I was not the same woman I had been just yesterday. It wasn't the faint pink spots all over my body, the love bites on my chest, or the way my sex looked, it was my eyes. They were different. They knew there was no going back for me.

Then I thought of my father. I quickly dressed and hurried down the stairs. As I neared the dining room, I heard him speaking in Russian to someone. I cornered the door and peeped in, I could see he was speaking to Gloria. He laughed at something she said before she took her leave.

It was time for me to go in but my legs refused to move. How would things be with us now?

"I can usually sense the presence of someone standing behind me," he said, his voice full of suppressed laughter.

Astounded at how awkward I was being, I walked in with a dry laugh.

"Hey," he said, looking exceptionally handsome this morning. He was dressed in a black t-shirt that seemed molded to the ridges of his chest, and a pair of dark pin-striped trousers framing the hips that had driven relentlessly into me the previous night.

"Hey," I said back.

For a moment, he held my gaze, then his eyes roved over the shorts and simple black tee I wore. He had seen me naked ... he knew exactly what I looked like underneath. I felt my cheeks flame.

Thank God, Gloria decided to make another appearance then.

She was carrying a pot of coffee. "Good morning," she called crisply, her smile and gaze kind.

I was more than grateful for the distraction as I returned the greeting.

Politely, she indicated towards the seat by Levan, where a place had been set.

It seemed as if Levan was drinking a coffee so dark it was almost black, but as if she knew exactly what I drank, she poured the filter coffee into my cup, and asked, "What would you like, dear? I can make you anything you want."

"Just anything that's available will do," I replied. "Thank you."

"Bring her a full English breakfast too," Levan said.

She nodded with a smile and left the room.

"Thanks," I said awkwardly. I wasn't used to having a man order breakfast for me. To seem more at ease and worldly and for something to do with my hands. I reached for an apple from a basket of fruits on the table, but as I did I saw four white, wooden boxes with Chinese or Japanese writing on them. "What are those?"

"Persimmons from Japan." He pushed one of the white boxes towards me. "Try one. They're rampant in Russia during the winter, but these ones are from a very special farm in Japan. They are supposed to be fifteen times sweeter than an ordinary persimmon."

I opened the box to find a single, perfectly shaped, flawlessly orange persimmon. It was carefully wrapped in straw and foam. It came with a pamphlet as if it was an expensive watch or designer assessor. "Oh, my God," I whispered, as I took it out of its protective packaging. I lifted it to my mouth and bit into it. Juices exploded in my mouth with some dripping down my chin.

It should have been embarrassing, but it was not. The persimmon was that good.

"Wow, I didn't expect it to be that soft," I said, reaching for my napkin. He didn't answer and my eyes rushed to meet his.

He was staring at me with an expression that was impossible to describe. Inside it was fierce possessiveness, a desperate hunger, tenderness and a dash of indulgence.

For a while, neither of us moved. We simply stared at each other with amazement. It was as if we were lost in a land of mutual appreciation.

Then Gloria appeared at the door holding a domed plate.

I tore my gaze away from his to look over at her. "Thank you," I said, my voice breathless, as she placed the plate in front of me. When she lifted the lid, the delicious smell of a cooked breakfast filled my nostrils. I put the fruit on the side plate then lifted my knife and fork. I was acutely aware of him watching my every move and it was making my whole body tingle as if there was a faint current of electricity under my skin. I wanted him to throw me on top of the table and flush my brains away once again.

"You mentioned something about my father?" I said, my voice sounding constricted and raspy.

"Eat something first," he said, his voice tight and strained.

I tried to ignore Levan's gaze on me as I cut into a sausage, but his proximity was messing with my mind and made my hands shake. To my horror, the fork fell from my grip and clattered noisily onto the table. Kicking myself internally, I picked it up.

"Are you alright?" he asked.

I nodded quickly. He didn't need to know that just listening to the sound of him breathing beside me was overheating my blood. "My father ..." I croaked out.

"What relations does he have to Meridian, Idaho?"

I paused for a moment to think. "None. Why?"

"He used his credit card in a convenience store down there."

My heart seized. "When?"

"Late last night. I got the report this morning."

I sat back then deep in thought. "Idaho? That's so far away. Why would he be ..." I stopped as something clicked. "My mom's nephew, Jeremy Sawyer used to live there. But for what reason would my father be there? They'd never really been friends, but after my dad cheated on my mom and it became public knowledge, everything was shot to hell."

"Perhaps they reconciled?" he said. "Maybe he has some business with him—"

"That's impossible," I interrupted. "Jeremy died two years ago. There's no reason he'd be there."

"He's dead?" he repeated.

"Yeah."

"And he didn't have any kids?"

I shook my head. "As far as I know, he didn't have any other family apart from us."

"Hmm."

"Well," I spoke again, "He did spend a little while in Idaho after he was released from prison, so it could be he has other contacts there."

"Don't worry about it. My men are checking it out even as we speak. They are thorough. If there is anything to be found, they will find it."

"But why would he be looking for anything in Idaho? Or was that where he planned to hide away after he sold me off?"

Levan didn't respond to my bitter snipe. Instead, he reached out and placed his hand on top of mine. His eyes communicated what he wanted me to feel, which was assurance, that all would be well in time.

I wanted to believe him, but there was so much I didn't know. "The woman ... that you and Aldie were speaking about yesterday. What was that about? I can't get it out of my head."

He let go of my hand.

At his reaction, my heart fell. "Levan."

"Bianca, just leave it."

"Aldie mentioned something about saving her ... is this related to me?"

"The less you know the better for you. I've got it handled," he dismissed the subject.

I wanted to insist, but his phone rang.

"I've got to take this," he said, and rising to his feet, walked away from the room.

I tried to return to my meal but my heart was too heavy.

It occurred to me then that I hadn't seen Biscuit around, so I headed into the kitchen and found Gloria talking rapidly in Russian to one of the maids.

They both stopped the moment I came in and looked at me with surprise. This was obviously not an area guests wandered into. "What can I do for you, dear?" Gloria asked politely.

"Um ... where's Biscuit?

"The gardener has taken him for a walk around the grounds," she replied.

"Oh, okay. I might do the same," I said awkwardly and quickly walked out of the room.

17

https://www.youtube.com/watch?v=qdoSy4ROZpg

A s I listened to Mikhail giving me his report about a matter unrelated to Bianca, I watched through the window, her trudge towards the stables, probably in search of her dog.

Telling her what she wanted to know would only serve to make her more worried than was needed. As she went out of my sight, I turned away and ended the call.

Just then, there was a sharp rap on the door. When I called *enter* Yuri came in, his face hard, and his gaze, stone-cold, the way it got when there was trouble.

"We know where they're keeping the boy."

Judging by Yuri's face that was not good news. "Where is he?"

"Right here in New Jersey."

I stared at him with astonishment. It didn't make sense. Why would Bogdan keep the boy in our backyard? "What?"

"Looks like Bogdan has become closely affiliated with the Death's Angels and he has asked them to keep him in their clubhouse. We guessed he was there purely from the fact of how much they've increased the security on their clubhouse these last few days, but this morning Marcus was finally able to get one of our guys in their Miami chapter to enter the premises. He confirmed they have the boy."

"Fuck!" I swore.

"Yeah. Death's Angels are insane. If we break in it'll be a damn blood bath."

I frowned. "Why the hell would they risk offending us to help Bogdan?"

He looked away for a moment.

My eyes narrowed at him. "What is it?"

He opened his mouth to speak, then hesitated.

"Fucking talk." I growled impatiently.

"They just elected a new president last November. Roman Tsepov. He was among Lazovsky's guys two years ago."

The moment he said the words, my chest throbbed with the memory of the four bullet wounds that had come so close to taking my life.

"After you were shot, your brother went on a rampage. He offed as many guys as he could from Lazovsky's gang. His brother was one of them. Since then, he's had a gun cocked at your family, so he's definitely not going to pass up this chance."

My phone rang. I pulled it out of my pocket to see that it was my brother. I pointed to the door for Yuri to leave and accepted the call.

Maxim's voice was as cold as ice. "Why didn't you tell me about Sarah Dale?"

"I'm handling it," I said, equally coldly.

"How?" he spat. "You want your head on a platter? Are you waiting till this all blows up so you can find out if Dad can really bear to bury his own son?"

"Maxim."

"You're risking your life and everything we have!" he roared. "Over a fucking woman."

He was right and he was wrong. "She's not just a woman," I said through gritted teeth. "She's my woman."

"Bogdan doesn't seem to think so and I tend to agree with him. The talk is, today is the last day he has given you to do so," he said. "Send her back to him. His little stunt is making the other dogs on the streets think that they too, can grow wings overnight and shit on us. If anything happens to that boy even by accident, and it just might happen with those lunatics he's given the boy to, then you and I are both dead."

I was silent for too long.

"You can't do it? You don't have the guts?" my brother grated harshly.

"Maxim, I'll take care of this. My way."

"You're running out of time," he said and cut the call.

I was left staring out of the window. I had a plan. I just had to stick to it. My phone rang. I took one look at the unidentified number and knew instantly who it was.

"My prince," Bogdan said, grating my nerves. "I've left you a little while without any disturbance, but I'm afraid you've failed to waltz as good as I expected. Your time is running out."

"Bogdan, you've grown a lot of balls."

"Never as big as yours, my prince. Never as big. I'm just trying to make you understand that your delay is dangerous and that there is a very important life in your hands. I'm sure you wouldn't want any harm to come to the child."

"I'm going to give you one last chance," I replied. "I'll pay you. Name your price."

He chuckled and I could hear the smugness in his voice. "Money? If money were the issue I would never have gone to these lengths. You understand me do you not? Why I need you to return the girl to me. It's the same reason why you felt the need to steal her from me in the first place. Desire is the deadliest of beasts. It catches a man in his chest and it claws into his body and sits inside like a ball of burning lava. It doesn't leave until you feed it." His voice suddenly changed, became hoarse with pure evil. "Give me the girl."

The hairs on my neck stood. I'd rather die than give Bianca to a monster like him. "No," I said.

"I heard that your brother's in town" His voice changed back, and sounded almost pleasant. "I have to say I am so close to wetting my panties to hear what he will have to say to you. He's a practical man. He knows what's good for business. I would listen to his advice if I were you. Return her to me by the end of the day, I'll release the boy, and we can all act like none of this ever happened."

"That would have been possible if you hadn't told the entire state why exactly you kidnapped the Solicitor General."

His laugh was giddy. "I got a little excited, but these things, they die down quickly."

"Well, I got a little excited too. Let's see which one of us will end up dead because of it." I ended the call and stormed out to the corridor outside.

Yuri was leaning against the wall and waiting on me.

"Call Chief Thompson and report the boy."

His eyes widened. "The Chief himself?"

"He's the only one right now with the authority to pull this off today. In the meantime, be on the lookout. They'll be trying to move the boy."

18

LEVAN

A few hours later, I was in the passenger seat of a blacked-out van with false number plates. We were parked just a few blocks away from the mid-east New Jersey club house. There were four other heavily armed men in the back ... in case things got heavy.

The Chief called and I immediately answered it.

"You're sure about this intel?" he asked worriedly.

"Absolutely," I replied confidently. Yuri was my father's best man. He was cautious to a fault and had never been wrong before.

"There'll be hell to pay if you're wrong," he muttered uneasily.

"I'm not."

"Right. Judge Williams just approved the warrant, so we're setting out now. I'll call you when it's over and give you an update."

"No need. I'm here and I have eyes on them."

"You're there?" he asked in surprise.

In this day of surveillance cameras in every damn doorway, my father, or brother would never be caught dead where the shit was going to go down.

But I was willing to risk being placed at the scene. Nothing was more important to me than saving Bianca. "Yeah, I'm here," I replied calmly.

"How does it look?"

"Uneventful. A couple of guys by the corner smoking ... a few bikes in the driveway ... and minimal movement."

"We'll be there soon."

Twenty minutes later, I heard the blast of sirens in the distance.

Soon, five patrol cars zoomed past us and screeched to a halt on the driveway of the house. About twenty officers jumped out of their vehicles fully armed. With precision, most of them moved to surround the premises while a few ran towards the door to demand entry.

My hands clenched and released around my cellphone. Once the boy was found and in our custody, I could take care of Bogdan. I dialed one of my men who was stationed at the back of the house. "Any movement, Alex?" I asked.

"No, boss. I can hear loud voices and panic all around, but no one's trying to escape the house. Maybe they found the boy and got them?"

Maybe, I responded in my head, but it sounded hollow. Something didn't feel right.

Soon, the cops began to exit the house and I sat up and put my hand out. "Binoculars?"

The device was placed on my palm, I held it to my eyes, and trained my sight on a bunch of bikers in handcuffs being escorted out of the house.

About twelve of them were brought kicking and screaming blue murder. They were thrown into the patrol cars. There was no child with them.

The blood was pounding in my ears. I knew there was no child even as I called the detective and he picked up on the first ring. "The boy?"

"We're still searching, but it doesn't look good. We've already done the cellar and attic and searched the garden for any trapdoors."

I cursed under my breath.

"Well, we'll keep on looking around for any clues of where they might have hidden the boy. Fortunately, there are other offenses lying around, so we'll get them for these, at least."

"Thanks, Thompson," I said and ended the call. My fist slammed onto the dashboard, cracking it and making pain radiate up my hand. The pain was welcomed. It was easier to handle than the intense frustration I felt. We had failed and worse—and worse, we had shown our hand to Bogdan. As we were driving away from the scene, my phone began to ring.

It was Bogdan. "You cheated, Prince. I thought you had more honor than that," he spoke the words without anger or emotion.

"Where's the boy?" I snarled.

"Safe, for now, but he is definitely going to pay for your mistake."

I heard the thrill of excitement running through his voice as he realized how deeply affected and out of control I was. He was right. I was so furious, so frustrated, and so fucking tied up in knots I couldn't even think straight anymore. Actually, from the moment I saw him with Bianca, I lost my head and started making erratic, highly emotional decisions. Each one compounding the situation ... making it more and more volatile.

I heard a loud smack through the phone and the child crying out in pain.

I closed my eyes, took a deep breath, and tried not to overreact. He was not going to hurt the child. Jacob was his Ace card. He would guard it with his life.

"Pull that trick just once more, and I'm going to start delivering pieces of him to you. I will start with his fingers. His grandmother will have you to keep providing for him, won't she? Which means he won't need them."

"Bogdan!" I roared, in spite of my better judgment.

"You're wet for me," he gloated with satisfaction. "Finally ... that's how I like my whores. Willing ... ready ... obedient."

"Bogdan, if you put your hands on that child, there will be no deal to be had. From anyone."

"Take a chill pill, kid," he said patronizingly.

His tone twisted my stomach into knots.

"I won't damage him too much. I wouldn't feel too good about it seeing that his grandmother was the one who called me to report what you were planning."

I stilled.

"Looks like you need to learn to keep the whores in your bed happy, Prince," he spat. "And to stay the fuck away from mine, otherwise I will make you bleed from the heart. I won't say this again!" He ended the call.

I instantly placed one to Sarah. "Why would you do that? Why would you tell Bogdan we were coming?" I asked incredulously, furiously.

"I told you not to try anything risky," she said, her voice shaking. "What if something had gone wrong and they had killed my grandson? And all over some stupid fight over some woman between the both of you. I am not taking that chance."

"Then do you want to take the chance that he forces you to expose everything by the end of today? It's not just your head on the line, I hope you realize this? We can find a way to get away from this but your career and legacy will be ruined. Not to mention you'll be behind bars and you'll never see Jacob again."

"I don't care about my legacy or my own freedom," she said.

"None of that matters. I just want my grandson back in one piece and I'll do whatever it takes to achieve that."

"Like what you did today?" I asked.

"You think I trust the police?" she nearly spat into the phone. "Those trigger-happy bastards will shoot first then ask questions. Bring my baby back to me, or I'll sing so hard and long I'll bring every one of you down."

https://www.youtube.com/watch?v=13iMsGNUHF0

I thought I might just go crazy in this big house. I needed to bake. Levan had disappeared right after breakfast and I hadn't laid eyes on him since.

It was a day off for the Chef, a mousy, grumpy man with a strong French accent.

Gloria had made lunch and gone out to run some errands. She said she would be back in a couple of hours.

The maids usually finished their cleaning by lunchtime and went back to their lives.

Of course, there was an army of dangerously armed guards outside and I could see a couple of gardeners toiling away at some garden beds, but I was basically all alone in this vast house.

Levan had a baker's dream for a pantry and I decided to keep myself busy, by trying out some recipes I'd always wanted to make for the store, but had never found the time.

The thought of my bakery saddened me. Francesca, one of the two girls who helped me in the store, had closed it down for me. It hurt to think of my store shut and a closed sign on it.

With a sigh, I left my room and began to head down the stairs, but as I arrived at the bottom step, the front door clicked open. My heart lodged in my throat when I saw Levan come in with two of his men. His face looked so hard and foreign I had to grab onto the banister by my side to keep myself standing.

He whirled around to his men, spat out what sounded like commands in Russian.

With a nod, both men took their leave.

Levan stood a moment longer with his back turned to me. His shoulders flexed, before he turned to face me. "How are you?" He looked slightly pale and a muscle kept ticking furiously in his jaw.

"Uh, alright," I answered uncertainly. "I was just heading over to the kitchen to do some baking."

"That's good," he said.

Then to my shock and astonishment, he turned to walk away.

My heart deflated like a balloon. After last night and this morning, I thought things between us would change. Now that we were both fully aware of the beautiful fire we could make together, we would become more intimate with each other, share more. But seeing him now ...

It was as if nothing had happened between us. We were like complete strangers. Had he already had enough of me? Impossible. I just could not accept or believe that. Not after last night. I needed to ask. I shouted to his departing back. "Are you alright? You seem," I searched for the word, "troubled."

He stopped at the sound of my voice, then turned slowly. "I'm fine. Just a little tired. I'll be fine." He forced a smile for me.

"Any word from your brother yet?"

His chest moved as he took a deep breath. "Yeah, I heard from him this morning. He's back in town."

"That's great," I replied awkwardly.

He frowned. "Look, I need to do something important. I'll meet you in the kitchen when I'm done." Without waiting for a response from me, he disappeared into his cavernous study down the hallway.

For a moment, I was too stunned to do anything, but stare after him in dejection, then I fished out my phone and called Aldie. She didn't pick up, and after three more tries, I left her a voice-mail. "Levan's acting weird and ... and that's not good, especially after last night. Freaking *call me,* and if I find out your phone died while you were in the store again, I'll kill you."

I headed off to the kitchen to search the pantry for ingredients. I got what I needed for my new rainbow cupcake creation, but at the last minute, I spotted the tall jar of pasta and grabbed that too. I decided then to make us a full dinner. Perhaps that would somehow bring us together again. Loosen the tense air between us.

Over an hour later, I had the cupcakes baking away in the oven and their lovely aroma filled the air. The pasta was boiling in water and in another pan, the Bolognese sauce the Chef had left in the fridge was simmering gently. With only a few minutes left for things to be concluded, it was time to invite Levan over. I went and knocked on his study door.

There was no response. I tried once more and was about to turn around.

His voice called through the door, "Come in."

I opened the door and saw him seated at the desk.

He was leaning back against his swivel chair, but the weird thing was, other than his phone, the surface of his desk was completely clean, as if he had just been sitting there doing nothing this whole time.

"I ... uh ... made some dinner and rainbow cupcakes. It's something I'm trying, but I'm not sure it will taste good. I kinda used some pretty unusual ingredients that I found in your Chef's pantry. You know, cinnamon, and lemon, and ..."

You're rambling!

I cleared my throat and got to the point, "I just wanted to say thank you for all you're doing for me. So there's dinner if you're hungry."

He didn't move while his expectant expression remained, as if he was waiting for something, or expected me to say more.

So, I ploughed on, "It's not a big deal what we did last night, and um … this morning so … uh … I hope we're okay." I was done talking and prepared to leave if he didn't throw me a bone too.

"We are,'" he said abruptly and rose to his feet. "Let's go eat this meal of yours."

"Sure," I said suddenly nervous. "I hope you like your meals spicy."

"Spicer than you like it," he said, picking up his phone from the desk to slip into his pocket.

I was confused. "How do you know that?"

His mouth quirked upwards. "Aldie, you, and I once played the spicy noodle game together, and I clearly remember you collapsed midway."

It hit me then, and boy, was I offended. "You're one to talk," I retorted. "I clearly remember you drinking a gallon of milk afterwards."

"I might have done that, but that was after I *won* the game."

He said this with such a smug chuckle it almost made me want to douse the whole pot with chili.

Then he walked around the desk, and the coldness left his gray eyes. They softened and darkened. He reached out and ran the back of his fingers down my cheek. "I can still remember how red your cheeks were that night. And how beautiful you looked."

I stopped breathing as all the hairs on my body stood to attention. We had not been this close to each other since this morning when he had ... I could feel my insides begin to melt, but I also knew my cupcakes would be good only for the trash can and the meal ruined if I stayed here much longer.

Still ...

His gaze lowered to my lips, then back up to my eyes.

I felt my heart start to beat wildly. My lovely cakes. What would my mother say if she saw me deliberately allowing good food to go to waste? A lifetime of lack and need pressed itself on my conscience. "Uh—I ..." My voice shook. "The food should be ready now. Could you help me set the table, please?"

"Sure," he replied, but there was a raw edge to his voice.

I tried to catch my breath as we walked together to the kitchen.

https://www.youtube.com/watch?v=xvvAYd3X5kA

"Since it's just the two of us," Levan said. "Why don't we eat at the counter?"

I glanced towards the inviting trio of high counter chairs by the island. "Sounds good," I agreed as I sprinkled fresh, finely chopped parsley over our steaming plates of minced beef and tomato sauce pasta.

"Looks amazing," he said as he came over to take the plates. He set them side by side on the counter.

I joined him with two bottles of water. "Cheese?" I asked.

He nodded.

I grated some parmesan over his food, then mine before

sitting next to him. "I hope it's good," I commented nervously.

"I hope so too." Picking up his fork, he dug in.

My heart felt as if it was damn well bouncing from one corner of my chest to the other, as I waited for his verdict.

"This may just be the best pasta I've ever had," he said.

I tightened my lips to hide how happy his compliment made me feel, but my reddening cheeks must have betrayed me. "Thank you," I mumbled, as I sneaked a glance at him.

We were so close together our shoulders were almost touching, the heat from the plates nothing to what I could feel sizzling between us.

"Why did you ask," he began, "if we were okay?"

Uh oh ... dangerous territory. "What do you mean?"

"Just now, in my study, after you said last night was no big deal, you asked if we were okay."

This might just be the last question I wanted to answer in any depth. My first thought was to chicken out, but then I straightened my shoulders and decided to push onwards. I didn't know how little time we had left together. So what if I got rejected ... again. Cowardice and shame were for people who were not staring death and destruction in the face. "Well," I swallowed, painfully wondering where the lump in my throat had suddenly come from. "When you came back this evening, you pretty much looked at me as if I was a complete stranger. Was last night just ... a one-time thing? An itch we needed to scratch?"

He made a strange sound. I couldn't tell if it was anger, frustration, or desperation, then his arm snapped around my waist in a strong grip. Before I could even gasp, he had pulled me to him. Then his lips swooped on mine.

It was the kiss of a starving man. It stole my breath away, my eyes clenched shut and my heart thundered in my chest as I went still.

Slowly, the kiss became buttery soft before he dragged his mouth away. "No matter what happens I want you to know ... I don't regret taking you and I never will. Nothing and no one can ever change that."

Dazed, I stared into his stormy eyes. My mouth hung open while my chest was heaving as I gasped for air. I felt as if the ground beneath me had given away.

He was watching me silently, in that hooded way of his, but it was as if he could see into my very soul.

I turned blindly away from him and focused my gaze on my plate. It looked blurry. I picked up the fork that had fallen from my hand.

He still hadn't answered me, not really.

I looked back at him and words tumbled out of my mouth, "I know about your family and everything and I'm not asking for a future with you, Levan. I just want to know what I am to you?"

He shot to his feet so fast, the stool fell back.

The sound, so loud in the empty space, I jumped. I said

nothing and watched him pace the kitchen floor restlessly, like a caged animal. It became clear he was in torment.

He held onto the edge of the counter, his head lowered towards the pile of dishes. "I've always wanted you," he muttered. He raised his head and looked at me. "From the moment I laid eyes on you, I couldn't get you out of my head. And last night ... last night I lost the fight. I couldn't hold myself back a moment longer. I went to you the way a heroin addict plunges a needle into his own fucking arm. There is nothing, nothing more important than what is in that needle to him. And even while the blood flows out of him, he is in ecstasy. That is what you are to me. Dangerous ecstasy."

I drew a shaking breath. The intensity with which he spoke left me in no doubt of his sincerity. "So now what?"

"To be with you, Bianca, in the way that we both want, I'll have to make a very hard choice."

"Haven't you already? You took me away from Bogdan."

"No, I haven't. That was the simple choice, because I'd rather lose my life than see any harm come to you."

My throat tightened. "What is more important than your life," I whispered.

"The hard choice," he admitted sadly, "is abandoning my world so that I can give you one that you deserve. Doing that will mean turning my back on the two people that mean the world to me. You will not understand it, because such things are alien in your world, but taking that step is tantamount to unforgivable betrayal."

I had absolutely no clue of what to say. I opened my mouth, but no words would come out. All I could do was call his name. That one word that expressed everything I could not say.

He came to me and I allowed his arms to engulf me. For the longest time, we remained in that spot, the undercurrents of sizzling passion and budding love making our blood hum. In his arms, there was so much that became brighter, so much I wanted to look forward to. So much I wanted to dream about and also so much I was afraid of. I pulled away and looked into his eyes. "I would never want you to give up your family."

"I know," he murmured gently. "You're very similar to my mother."

That came out of left field. "What?" I asked, unsure whether I should be flattered or insulted. Neither he nor Aldie had ever mentioned her before and to my shame, I had always been so enamored by him I'd never thought to ask either. I didn't even know if she was still alive.

"Both of you have the same temperament," he explained. "Kindhearted, soft, but extremely strong headed. You chart your own rules without apology, and you only bend it for one thing. Love. Others can walk away when the going gets hard, but not you. Not when you've made a commitment. Even if that will spell a life of misery. Then you'll carry on even if you can barely stomach the grief. Even if it kills you. I don't want to do that to you."

I couldn't believe how much he *saw* me. It terrified me. No matter what, I didn't want to lose him.

He kissed me again, hard and desperate.

I lost myself in him. My emotions were running high, bubbling dangerously. Tears misted in my eyes as I savored the taste of this man who I wanted like no other, desired like nothing else.

We broke apart, our breathing ragged.

He rested his forehead against mine. "I need you," he said. "More than you can possibly understand, but I am afraid I will hurt you. It'll kill me if I do that to you."

"Levan ..." My voice was barely a whisper. "The only way you can hurt me is when you give me the impression you don't care."

"Don't care? If only you knew. Day and night I have to hold myself back because all I want to do is fuck you until you pass out."

With a little laugh, I buried my face in his neck and pounded lightly on his broad, strong chest. "I didn't pass out," I muttered in defense. "I was exhausted and I had barely even eaten all day."

"Well, you've just eaten now ..." he taunted softly.

I lifted my gaze at the challenge. The look in his eyes would be something I would remember forever. The promise of relieving pure and ethereal bliss once more snaked between us, tantalizingly. My spine rattled with a shiver.

I crushed my mouth to his and welded my body against his. His hands clawed into my hair as he held my head in place. Then he, he ... *worshipped* me with his tongue. There was no other way to describe what he did. Teasing, stroking, licking, sucking and showing me beyond what words could express just how deeply and intensely he craved me.

His scent was intoxicating, the memory of the previous night making my heart pump so hard, I felt as if it would burst. The sweet pleasure became so intense my coherence began to slip. I dove for the fine buttons of his shirt and pulled at them. My fingers were so hasty and desperate they caused more of a delay than I could bear. So I went to the zipper of my shorts. I pushed them down my hips. As they slid down my legs, I immediately hurried to his belt, jerking the leather out of its loop.

He palmed me, his hand warm and hard through the soft cotton of my underwear.

It drew a long, tortured moan out of me.

"You're soaked," he muttered in my ear, "and we only just started."

I moved my hips frantically against his palm. "These days ... my mind doesn't seem to want to think about much else other than you and the things you do to me. I am constantly wet," I admitted hoarsely.

He pulled back and gazed into my eyes.

"And ready ..." I breathed.

His gaze glued to mine, he slid the crotch of my panties aside and slipped a finger inside of me.

Pure molten desire flowed from my sex into my body. "Desperate for you to ..." I trailed away as his thumb stroked the swollen bud of my arousal with just the perfect amount of pressure and in a precise circular rhythm that completely drained all the blood from my head. "Oh, F-fuck," I gasped helplessly.

Another finger joined his assault and my eyes closed shut. I was limp against him as he began to thrust roughly into me. My arms went around him. It felt as if my whole body was pulsating and throbbing with the primal need for release.

The crazy sensations coursing inside me were probably compounded by the dangerous situation we were in. Now I was starting to understand my growing love for him, for the way that he prioritized my wellbeing above all else.

In his arms, I found the kind of pleasure that left me hanging onto my sanity by a thread. I lifted my leg to grant him even deeper access. My back arched and I could feel the hard muscles of his forearm digging into my body as he held me up and against the force of his other hand's thrusts.

While his fingers pummeled me hard and fast, he swooped down on my lips, and plunged his tongue into my mouth. I sucked it hungrily until I climaxed right there, in his kitchen. The walls of my sex clenched greedily around his fingers as my hips jerked erratically at the force and heat of my release. It vibrated through me ...thick, strong and delicious. When my knees buckled at the ecstasy coursing through me, I hung onto him.

He didn't let up until he'd milked every ounce of pleasure out of me.

I collapsed into him, spent and satiated, the beat of my heart in overdrive as heat radiated through me. The rush was humbling. I knew there would never be anyone in my life to move me the way he did. I had suspected this from the day I'd set eyes on him in my bakery, but now I knew.

In the past, I could only imagine this degree of intimacy with him, but after the taste he had given me of what it meant to be fucked thoroughly and wholly by Levan Ivankov, no man would ever measure up to him.

He would be mine and I was going to do all in my power to ensure it.

I kissed him deeply and then pulled away to say in the most seductive voice I could, "Now, I will be the one to turn you into jelly."

His smile crept across his yummy lips slowly and as sexy as fuck.

It made my heart skip several beats. My hands went back to that damn belt of his. It was too secure.

With an odd growling chuckle that didn't sound anything like real amusement, he pushed away my ineffective effort and unbuckled it in one smooth movement.

Immediately, I grabbed onto the tab of his zipper and yanked it down. Shoving his white briefs down, I enveloped his thick, rock-hard shaft in my hands. My mouth watered with giddy anticipation as I locked my gaze with his.

His eyes were hooded and almost midnight-black with lust.

I dropped to my knees on the cold granite floor. First, I lapped at the pearl of pre-cum that appeared on the tip. Then I stretched my lips over the massive, throbbing head of his cock. I gave it a long hard suck and felt the breath hiss out of him.

"*Fuck*," he cursed softly.

Smiling devilishly at the effect I was having, I took as much of him as I could into my mouth. I felt his head move all the way in and hit the back of my throat. Lightly, I grated my teeth along the sensitive flesh as I drew back out.

Settling my hand around him in a hard grip, I began to fist him, lifting the column of desire up to suck gently on his balls. His moan was like music to my heart.

I returned my attention to the wide crown and settled into a delicious rhythm as I firmly stroked him from root to tip. I watched him reach out to hold onto my head, but at that moment, I slipped his wide crown into my mouth.

His hands curled and froze mid-air at the potent pleasure. "Ahhh," he breathed as he threw his head backwards, his legs widening even further to accommodate me.

I hollowed my cheeks and started to really blow him then.

"Oh, Bee," he called, and the name, especially in the current context was so sweet, I took him deeper than I had taken any man. When his hands found their way to my head to guide me, I was ready. I wanted him to fuck my mouth. I wanted him to climax as hard as I did. I helped him chase his release by sucking harder.

Perhaps I pumped him too eagerly because he immediately began to quicken, his hips jerking with increased urgency.

It made me feel proud to see him so vulnerable. He tried to

pull away when he came, but I gripped his firm buttocks and kept all of him in my mouth, and kept on sucking him.

"Bianca," he roared into the night, as his hot cum shot into my throat.

I sucked him dry, drinking it all eagerly and giggling like a daft teenager afterwards. It was almost embarrassing how much I enjoyed the taste of him.

A hand slipped around my neck and his gaze bored into mine. It was filled with sheer wonder as he pulled me up to him and kissed me. "How are you real?" he whispered, before he continued to drown me in his taste.

I was quite dizzy when I broke away from him, and reached for his buttons. I didn't need to worry if my trembling fingers could work those fine buttons, because he grabbed the front edges and ripped the shirt open. Buttons flew all over the kitchen. After he casually shrugged his shirt off his shoulders, he stood still and seemed unable to take his piercing gaze away from me.

It made me feel like the luckiest prey alive.

His shirt was off but before I could do much about it, he grabbed me once more and placed me against the counter with my back to him. Without complaint, I ground my naked ass against him, writhing my wet flesh against his hardening cock. "Levan," I breathed. "I can't wait."

He slipped it between the soaking folds of my sex as I held onto the edge of the counter and waited for the delicious intrusion. My hands fisted and pounded upon the counter, as the walls of my sex convulsed with the need to clench around him and milk the both of us for the pleasure. I couldn't bear it any more. I had to feel him moving inside me. "Fuck me, Levan," I breathed, but it sounded more like a growl in my ears.

He parted my folds with one hand, sliding his fingers up my dripping slit, and taunting the taut tortured bud that rested at the top. When I thought I would die from pleasure, he slipped into me. My back arched with pure bliss. He thrust the rest of himself into me, hard, and it shoved my hips against the counter.

"Oh fuck," he swore at his complete possession of my body.

I writhed seductively against him in response. I turned to look at him and my soul almost left my body.

"Oh, my God!" I screamed.

21

LEVAN

I froze at her sudden piercing cry.

"What the fuck?" I exclaimed, trying to grab her arms to find out what was wrong, but she had already slipped away from my cock and was crouched down to the floor to hide herself.

My blood started boiling. The interruption was intolerable. Somebody had come in at a very wrong time and he was going to pay for it. "Who the fuck is that?" I roared, as I lifted my gaze to the door.

A man stood very still at the doorway.

Maxim.

My heart slammed into my chest.

Fuck. Fuck. Fuck

"I apologize for the intrusion," he said, without an ounce of real apology in his voice.

With a hard look at him I crouched down next to Bianca, her eyes looked enormous with embarrassment. I pressed a kiss on her forehead. "I'm sorry sweetheart, it's my brother."

"I'll let you both finish," Maxim said from the doorway.

As his footsteps died away, my balls felt painfully heavy, and my entire abdomen was taut with the need for release, but the moment was completely gone. Truth was I shouldn't even have been doing what I was doing. Not with what was at stake. Gently, I pulled her back up. "I'm sorry, but I have to go talk to him," I said, brushing golden strands of hair out of her face.

"No, it's fine. Go ahead," she replied with a small smile.

I could tell she was still visibly shaken. While she reached for her clothes, I quickly pulled up my pants. Then I pressed a kiss to her cheek, and was on my way to the study.

I went into the study, shut the door behind me, and turned to face him. "You came to scare her into the grave?" I gritted my teeth.

"Sorry," he said in Russian.

I breathed deeply and tried my best to dissipate the anger I felt.

"You're still excited," he said sarcastically. "Go finish up and get right back here. I need to show you something."

"Fuck you," I snarled.

He grinned. "Well, well ..."

I had a good mind right at that moment to knock the son of a bitch out. "Get on with it."

"Bogdan just sent this."

Something in his tone made me turn around, the hairs on my neck standing. With a frown, I headed over to the computer and looked at the video that was on the screen.

Maxim pressed the play button.

What I saw on the screen made my blood run cold. For the first time in my life, I felt real fear. It crawled over my skin like a god damn spider. I could feel the blood drain from my face as every nerve in my body contracted and shuddered. I actually felt cold.

Oh, fuck.

"Do you know her?" Maxim asked.

It was hard to speak. I swallowed hard and balled my hands into fists. "I do. That's Bianca's best friend, Aldie." I turned away from my brother's hard, searching eyes and picked up my phone. I saw all the frantic missed calls that had come in while I was enjoying myself with Bianca. I nearly winced with shame and fury at my own incompetence. With my heart pounding, I called Yuri back.

"What's going on?" I asked urgently.

He didn't answer immediately and more paralyzing fear pumped into me. "What is it?" I roared.

"The girl ... Aldie. Bogdan's men took her. They came in full force. All the hired mercenaries are dead and two of our men are injured. It's bad. There are police everywhere."

"How long ago was this?" I asked as I replayed the video again, my gut twisting as if a knife had been stuck in it to see the terror in Aldie's face.

"Half-an-hour now."

I ended the call and dialed Bogdan. The fear was gone. All that was left was a deadly calm. Bogdan had picked the wrong man to play his games with. He had underestimated me. Yes, I was young. Yes, I was inexperienced. Yes, I was not an insane psychopath like him. But he had forgotten the golden rule. A little sewer rat can be more dangerous than a cobra when it is cornered. It can fly up and sink its teeth right into your jugular. And while you are bleeding out, it will go right back to being just vermin.

"My Prince," he answered. "I was just about to throw the girl to my dogs. I thought perhaps I captured the wrong pawn and you didn't give a damn whatsoever about her."

"Bogdan," I stated quietly. "You must be aware that the only reason you're still alive is because I've allowed it, but if you hurt one hair on that woman's head, your body will hang from the Brooklyn Bridge."

A few seconds passed before he responded, "You pushed me today, Levan, and I'm not going to let it go. Consider your time up. Tomorrow morning the Solicitor General will announce to the whole world how your family has had her and half of the law enforcement in the country at your bidding, or I will kill the boy. You and your family are finished, Levan," he spat. "Oh, and I'll give you one more day to return the woman you stole from me. Otherwise, I'll deliver her best friend here in pieces to your doorstep." He ended the call.

I slowly lowered the phone from my ear.

"The deadline's in ..." Maxim glanced at his watch. "Six hours, but you don't seem to be worried at all about missing it."

"It's ended now," I said flatly.

Maxim rose to his feet. "What!"

I lifted my gaze to meet his and he saw exactly what I wanted him to see.

He shook his head in wonder, "You're prepared to hand us over, aren't you?" His voice sounded far too calm. "In exchange for her."

"We'll survive," I said. "She won't."

"And what makes you think that *you* will? If Dad doesn't put a bullet into that thick head of yours, I fucking will."

"Go ahead," I said, and turned around towards the door.

"Come back here," he commanded.

I yanked the door open and went into the hallway.

"Levan!" he shouted.

I was just about to reach the front door when a heavy hand landed on my shoulder. He spun me around and drove his big fist into my face. The blow was so powerful it felt as if my jaw had caved in from the force of it. I was thrown against the door. Pain wracked through my head, blinding me, making me see stars.

I took a few moments to recover and when my hand went to my face it came away with flowing blood from what I was certain was my now broken nose. With a sigh, I staggered to my feet and turned to gaze at my brother. "Let's get this over with."

The veins on his forehead visibly throbbed with fury, but his blue gaze was filled with something that looked like disappointment. He pounded his fists into my stomach and I let him. In fact, I welcomed them. I knew I deserved his rage and I was truly sorry for the mess I had brought onto my family, but I just couldn't let Bianca go.

Anything but that—I would rather die.

My brother was big and strong and his punches were crushing. I was left reeling, gasping. I doubled over, the wall against my back.

In the distance, I heard Bianca scream, "Stop it. Stop it! You're going to kill him."

I shouted back to her, "Stay away. Don't come any closer."

Her voice triggered something in Maxim as he drew back and looked down at me while I collapsed to the ground, my arms wrapped around my bruised rib cage. "I'm going to go clean up your fucking mess," he swore at me. "And then I'm going to come for you." With that, he turned around and stormed out of the house.

I couldn't help the smile that bubbled up to my face. I had gotten off easy.

22

BIANCA

I watched, struck with horror at what was going on.

As his brother slammed the door, I ran towards Levan.

He was lying on the floor bloodied and battered, almost in a fetal position.

The sight drove a chill so cold up my spine, the little hairs I had never seen on my back stood up.

His brother was the fiercest man I had ever laid eyes upon, and it had very little to do with his build although that was nerve racking enough.

It was in everything else about him ... his gaze ... piercing and almost crippling... the tone of his voice as though he held dominion over every single person and thing he came upon. His stance was authoritative and assertive even when he wasn't speaking.

Levan was quite similar to him in all of these regards, but

something about Levan was unmistakably different. That something was kindness. It shone in his eyes, his smile, his voice. It made him approachable.

That note of humanity seemed to be completely absent in his brother. Levan commanded admiration and respect at first glance, while Maxim, was unsettling in the darkest of ways. He seemed like a man who had seen more darkness than you ever wanted to know existed.

For a moment there, I had been certain he would kill Levan. My heart was pounding ferociously in my chest. "Levan!" I cried, as I crouched next to him.

Even as his gaze turned to me the front door suddenly burst open and his men rushed in. I halted in my tracks as they rushed over to him.

He gave his orders to them in Russian, but his gaze remained on me as they lifted him to his feet.

I couldn't move. I was so shocked.

"Stay here and wait for me," he said, but his voice was so low, I wasn't certain if I heard the actual words, or just seen the movement of his lips.

I was still standing there frozen to the spot when the door banged shut.

At the resounding silence that followed, goosebumps broke out across my skin. I looked around the massive and empty house I had been imprisoned in, and felt utterly useless. While everyone else seemingly fought for me, I had no clue as to what was going on. All while, no one even felt like I needed to know. I ran my fingers through my hair in stunned confusion.

With a heavy sigh, I headed back into the kitchen. I walked to the counter and sat on one of the stools. I stared at the oven blankly. I felt sick to my stomach.

Suddenly, I was running to the sink, my body jerking as it tried to vomit out the poison I had seen and heard. First the half-digested pasta, then bitter bile came out. Tears were pouring from my eyes. I leaned heavily against the sink as my body tried to find some equilibrium again. But all I found was fear.

Terrible, terrible fear for Levan.

My hands started to shake. I closed my eyes and tried to think rationally.

I needed to speak to Aldie, now, more than ever. I ran to the counter, snatched up my phone and dialed her number ... once again, the call didn't go through. There was no way she would have been this off grid for so long. She was addicted to her phone.

The last time I had panicked, allowed fear to take over, and overreacted. This time I wouldn't let myself do that. Levan's men were guarding her. Maybe she lost her phone. Or she had let it run out of battery again. Yes, that was probably it.

Even so, I tried a couple more times, but when there was still no response, my instincts started screaming at me. I felt it was time to get Levan involved, but after the last time I didn't want to be the boy who cried wolf either, especially since it was obvious he had something grievously serious going on between him and his brother. I wasn't oblivious to the fact that it definitely had something to do with the mess I had brought into their family.

Torn with the need to make sure Aldie was really okay and the desire not to put more stress on Levan, I paced the floor restlessly. I stopped and stared out of the window. The world outside seemed full of danger. I was safe in here, but Aldie was out there. She didn't ask for any of this.

I dialed his number and waited for his phone to ring. When it did, he did not pick up. Frowning, I dialed again. After a few more tries, I suspected he was ignoring me on purpose, but instead of going off the deep end, I calmed myself down with the thought that in his battered state it was even possible that he wasn't even aware of the whereabouts of the phone. I looked towards the study and realized that the door had been left wide open from the squabble they just had.

I walked in like a zombie. I had never snooped on anyone before, but I knew Levan was keeping things from me. It was his way of protecting me, but I needed to know. Perhaps something would give me a clue as to what had caused the sudden brawl between him and his brother. It was absolutely unexpected based on what Levan had told me so far, his brother was well aware of him rescuing me from Bogdan. It made me realize I hadn't been told the whole story.

With the kind of activities the Ivankovs were involved in I doubted there would be anything incriminating left out to be found, but I swept my gaze around nevertheless. My eyes instantly fell on an open laptop sitting on the desk. I walked over to it. I expected to see a black screen, ready to ask for a password – but for some weird, totally insane reason, as if the angels themselves wanted me to know – the screen was frozen on a video.

It wasn't possible to see it clearly, but it looked like there was a barefoot, but clothed woman sitting on a dirty concrete floor. Her head was covered with a bag, so I couldn't see her face, but I could see her hands were tied behind her back.

With shaking hands, I pressed the play button.

A sharp command was being given in Russian. Then two men began to march towards the girl.

"Don't come near! Don't fucking touch me!" she screamed in English.

My jaw dropped and my heart seized. Aldie ... Jesus Christ. *The bound girl with the bag on her head was my Aldie!*

One of the men pulled the bag away from her head and like a striking snake, she threw herself forward and sunk her teeth into him. He roared with pain and fury. What followed was a slap so heavy it flung her across the floor. She screamed, and the sound went right through me. I had never heard her scream before. My hand reached out to the screen in despair as I watched her lay there, unmoving while my other hand rushed to cover my mouth.

What if that brute had broken her neck?

Then I saw her move and a whimpering sound rose from her prone body. The man came back and grabbed Aldie roughly by her hair. He jerked her head up mercilessly and held her in place whilst the camera began to move. All the men were masked so I couldn't see any of their faces but hers.

Her mouth moved, but no sound came out.

Rapid Russian was blasted out along with wild, unrestrained laughter of the other men in the room.

Then the screen went black.

Oh, God! Aldie.

23

"Do we need to visit the hospital?" Yuri asked, as we reached the gates.

I met his gaze in the rearview mirror. Removing the blood-soaked face towel from my nose, I noted the way it was swollen and quickly becoming blue-black, but I was so hyped up I didn't feel any pain at all. "I'm fine," I said and leaned back.

Alex in the passenger seat beside Yuri turned, concern in his gaze. "Your nose is definitely broken. Let's make a quick stop."

"No! What we need is to find Bogdan now. He's confident that Aldie is more than enough leverage, but what he doesn't know is that Maxim is on his trail and he doesn't give a shit about her. If Maxim gets to him before we do ... Aldie will become collateral damage."

"We've been searching for Bogdan since he took the child and we've had no luck," Yuri said. "And anytime we get a lead, he seems to somehow slip out of our sight again, the fucking bastard." Yuri looked ashamed to make this admission.

"Maxim has eyes on everybody that needs to be monitored," I reminded my men. "Unless Bogdan is a ghost, Maxim will be able to locate him within the hour."

The silence in the air grew suddenly heavy and I immediately understood why. It was perhaps even harder to find my brother unless he wanted to be found.

"How do we find the boss?" Alex asked quietly.

I pulled my phone out of my pocket and searched through it for my brother's tracker. We had had enough scares as a family over the years, and after my last near death dance with bullets, he had put trackers on all of us. Everyone in our family wore a ring with our family insignia of a cross, an anchor, and a heart engraved into it. It was also equipped with a homing device.

"Greenwich Village," I said. "106 Macdougal Street."

"Got it," Yuri said as the gates closed behind us.

As the car sped on, I looked at the address again. It was quite familiar, but I couldn't place why. I lifted my head and looked at my men. "Do any of you know this place?"

"I do," Yuri answered. "It's Arturo's Mexican restaurant, El Parador."

"Arturo Guzman?"

"Yes," Yuri replied. "He has an underground hideout there for any dealings which Maxim ensures stays off grid."

I scowled. "New York is my jurisdiction. Why am I just hearing about this?"

"It all happened way before you officially joined operations. When we were still on the streets with Gennady. Then Arturo and I used to work for Maxim. Arturo took a bullet for him once and Maxim has helped him out ever since then."

In half an hour, we arrived at the street. Yuri slowed down a few yards away from the Mexican restaurant. Despite the ungodly hour of 2:53 a.m., the streets were still bursting with people in the neighborhood. Jazz bars and comedy venues still welcomed patrons while prostitutes both male and female casually strolled down the street.

"Don't go too close," I warned.

"No, boss," Alex said, stopping near a Mongolian bakery.

"Arturo has spies almost everywhere in the country," Yuri said. "If anyone can find Bogdan, it'll be him."

A few minutes later a few figures appeared from behind the Mexican grill and I instantly recognized the tall erect figure of my brother. In his expensive dark suit and buzz haircut, he stood out in this scummy neighborhood.

He spoke quickly to the shorter man whom I assumed was Arturo, while the other group of three men went ahead and jumped into the waiting SUV. Maxim ended his brief chat and got into the car.

"Follow him," I instructed. "From a distance." Blood suddenly trickled down my nose onto my clothes. With a curse, I grabbed the towel I had tossed aside once again and held it to my nose. I kept my eyes on the road as we followed silently behind Maxim, but the adrenaline was leaving my bloodstream and pain had begun to radiate through my body. My head felt as if it was splitting into jagged pieces. I had to shut my eyes at the impending nausea and hazy vision.

"He's slowing down ..." Alex said.

I heard him but couldn't make my eyes open. I leaned back against the headrest and muttered out my instructions, "Let me know when they stop, and disembark."

We continued on the road until a few minutes later when Alex called, "Boss."

"Yeah?" Even speaking was hard. My whole stomach and ribcage area felt as if they were on fire.

"They just got out, and about a dozen of our guys are waiting. They're all armed."

I shot up then, my vision instantly clearing up as I focused my gaze through the windshield.

"That's Sergei," Yuri pointed out. "Viktor and Otari ..."

I nodded blankly, the reality of what was about to happen beginning to dawn on me. "Maxim's going to end him."

24

BIANCA

I was distraught as I ran out of Levan's study in horror. I stood in the sumptuous hallway in a state of complete shock and confusion. Nothing seemed real anymore. It was like I was caught in a nightmare. Everything I thought and believed was a lie.

Levan knew and he didn't tell me!

Moments passed as I stood there in limbo. Not knowing what to do, what to think, how to help Aldie. Tears stung my eyes at the thought of the way that man had hit her. The way she had flown across the room as if she was no more than a ragdoll.

I shook with *rage* ... if any one of them laid a filthy hand on her, I was going to kill them all myself. I pushed the blind fury back. This was not the time to fall apart or act stupidly. With every second I remained here, she drew closer to her death. I knew what Bogdan was capable of.

At the traffic lights that first night after he took me, I'd seen into the eyes of the monster that lived inside him. The fear of what he might do to her was crippling. This storm was my fault and it was up to me to make it better.

I took a deep breath. *Think Bianca, think.* I simply couldn't stay locked up here then find out that everyone I gave a fuck about had been killed. I needed to get out of here and find a way to help her, but there was no way out. The place was more guarded than a prison. I went over to the window by the front door, and peeped outside. I saw no one, and for a moment, it gave me hope.

Perhaps they'd all left with Maxim and Levan. No, impossible ... Levan would not leave me unguarded.

Nonetheless, I pulled the door open and stepped out onto the marble porch. I looked past the compound of perfectly manicured plants and flower beds towards a high iron fence. I knew I could climb it, as long as it wasn't electrified. I took another step, walking towards it. No one came to ask me what I was doing and I began to wonder if perhaps the house was truly empty. I couldn't believe my luck. Perhaps this would be easier than I thought.

I threw a little branch at the fence to see it sizzle and crackle.

Right, it was electric.

I turned to run towards the gate. A few minutes later, I reached it. I slowed down to a walk and looked nervously around. There was still no one in sight. I realized however with a sinking heart that the massive gate was locked and probably centrally controlled.

As I was contemplating my options, a shadow fell on me. I was so startled I shrieked and jumped away.

"Is there a problem, Miss?" It was one of the guards. He had a thick Russian accent, cold black eyes, no smile, and a black gun in his hand.

I looked to the left and right as I wondered where the fuck he had come from. He had *literally* appeared out of nowhere. "Uh ..." I began. "Uh ... no."

He loomed over me like a brick wall as he stated clearly, "Then please go back to the house."

I wanted to argue. I wanted to tell him to open the gates and let me out, but I knew he wouldn't. It would be certain death for him most likely and nothing I did or said would make him turn from his purpose. I turned around and hurried back to the house. My heart was pounding in my chest as I shut the door solidly behind me.

It would be impossible to leave here so easily. Of course it was—I needed a better plan.

25

LEVAN

I was surprised when Maxim and his men actually arrived at their destination.

It was a freaking mart in Sheepshead bay. The front was filled with fruit and vegetable carts. Given the late hour, there were only a few people going in and out of the store.

"Move!" I ordered my men, and we all got out of the car.

The men walked into the mart to the widened gaze of the few patrons browsing the aisles. Maxim and the men had disappeared from sight. I pulled out my phone from my pocket and called Maxim as my guys spread out to find the entrance to what must obviously be an underground unit.

Maxim didn't pick up.

I tried again, trying my best to keep calm and pray he wouldn't make a mistake that even I would never be able to forgive him for.

"Found it, Boss!" Alex called.

Clutching my ribs, I hurried with him past the counter of the small food service station through the door that Maxim and his men must have disappeared behind.

As I went down the stairs, I heard roars and grunts of pain down the bottom of the narrow stairs.

Just as I arrived at the bottom, someone was thrown into the door at the base. The door flew off its hinges with the weight of the man. He lay mangled at my feet.

One of Maxim's guys, Otarim arrived at the door. His gun was pointed at us, until he recognized us. Then his eyes widened in shock and he instantly put his weapon away. "Boss." He gave a deep bow to show he was sorry.

More men came running towards us. When they saw me, they parted and made way for me, so I could move through the doorway.

"Where's the girl?" I asked, stepping over the prone man.

One of the men jerked his head towards the interior of the room.

I walked into the room I'd seen in the video. There were about eight more men in that storage room. My gaze instantly went to Aldie, still bound, her eyes widened in shock at the sight of me.

Three other men were on the ground ... two unconscious ... one with his head busted open and a pool of blood around it. Another of Bogdan's men was on his knees with his hands knitted behind his head. I looked around and found Maxim in the shadows, his arms folded across his chest, as he leaned against a wall. His eyes were veiled, but he was watching me. As if this was a test to see what I would do.

One of Maxim's men went to Aldie, perhaps to help her, but I lashed out in Russian. He jumped back in fright, his gaze moving between me and Maxim, as if he couldn't understand what he was supposed to do.

I went over to Aldie and carefully pulled the duct tape off her mouth.

Tears rolled down her eyes. "Levan ..." she cried, her chest rising and falling.

"It's alright. I'm here now. Nothing can hurt you."

"Levan," she howled, and there was a note of accusation in her voice, as if she had trusted me and I betrayed that trust.

"I'm so sorry, Aldie." I pulled her into a hug.

She sobbed uncontrollably against my chest.

I shut my eyes, my chest tightening in pain at the trauma she had gone through. "Are you hurt?" I whispered as I patted her back. "Did they touch you?"

She shook her head.

I sighed with relief even though obvious bruises told a different story and reached to pull her up. "We need to leave before Bogdan's men return."

She immediately shot to her feet and turned around, so I could undo the ties that bound her hands together.

"Alex!" I called. "I need a knife."

He came into the room to hand one over.

I set her free with it. "Take her to the car," I said.

She grabbed onto my arm, reluctant to leave me.

"It's fine," I assured her, my gaze on hers. "I'll be right there."

She went with Alex.

I turned to face my brother.

He had only one question for me, "What's your plan, little brother? You're still going to burn us all for that woman?"

I turned around and walked out of there, leaving a place that smelt of death and torture.

26

BIANCA

I figured out what to do and I was certain it would work. I called 911.

"I can't breathe," I croaked to the operator, making my voice weak and breathless. "I think I'm about to pass out."

"Can you give me your location?" the operator asked calmly.

"105, Norwood Avenue, Elberon. Help. Please help me," I gasped dramatically and ended the call before she could extract any more information. Rushing to the foyer, I threw myself to the ground. I knew I had to look ill enough to warrant the call.

Within twenty minutes, I heard the sirens approaching, but to my shock they stopped.

I panicked.

Perhaps the guards had stopped them at the gate. Luckily,

the door flew open then. I conjured up a grimace of pain as I lifted my gaze to the two guards that stood at the doorway.

At the sight of me on the floor, they rushed over. It was clear they had no idea what to do. "What's wrong, Miss? What's going on?" Full of concern they tried to lift me up.

I just sealed my eyes and played dead.

I remained limp as they checked my pulse and spoke urgently to each other in Russian. Through my eyelashes, I could see one of them pull his cellphone out. I assumed he was going to contact Levan. I knew then I needed to be out of here before he found me. To distract him, I began to wail pitifully.

Just then, I heard the door fling open again.

Paramedics dressed in hi-visibility vests and bright orange emergency kits burst in.

I didn't say a word as they tried to get me to speak to them. It worked. I was quickly put on a stretcher, carried out of the house, and placed into an ambulance.

I kept my face contorted in pain as I was driven out of the compound. I was certain the guards were following close behind.

When we arrived in the emergency room, the questions about what was wrong with me abounded from every corner and yet, I didn't give a response.

Then the doctor inspected me, a stethoscope to my chest ... and a penlight to my pupils.

I needed to end this before I got caught.

I held onto the doctor's hand and made a simple request, "I need to use the—bathroom," I pleaded in a broken voice.

He looked confused and just a bit ticked off. "What?"

"I need to use the bathroom."

"Sure," he said a little shocked, and took a step back.

The nurse in attendance took over. "Can you walk?"

I nodded and with her help, I slowly rose to my feet.

As I walked away supported by her, I couldn't help but notice all the other true emergencies that filled the room. For a second, the sight twisted my heart with guilt, but my best friend's life was on the line. I had nothing to apologize for.

She guided me into the restroom and the moment we were alone, I turned to her. "Please help me," I pleaded. "Can you take me somewhere those men who came with me can't follow, please?"

Her eyes narrowed, part confusion part suspicion, before they widened with understanding and hardened into twin lights of determination. "Do they have you against your will?"

"Uh … not really. Usually I like them around but not tonight." Then I realized I was sounding like some spoilt rich brat that was trying to evade the protection her insanely wealthy father had arranged for her, so she could slip away and party. "I need to be away for something very, very urgent, and important. Please, my best friend's life depends on it."

Now, she looked confused again.

"Please help me," I cried. "I beg of you."

"Does this mean then that you're fine?" she asked.

My heart dropped into my stomach with shame. "Yes, I'm fine, but it was the only way I could get away to help my friend. I'm so sorry."

She didn't seem very happy with me anymore and I didn't blame her, but I was lucky. She pressed on, "And you're sure you don't want me to call the cops? This doesn't sound good at all."

"No, trust me under normal ... well, what's normal for me these days? I'd need them by my side."

She sighed then and looked away in contemplation. "Those men out there look pretty tough. You're putting me in a real situation young lady. I hope you know what you are doing."

"I do and thank you so much for this," I said quickly.

"Right, I'll take you for uh ... perhaps a CBC test. We should be able to get away then."

My eyes misted with gratitude. "Thank you so much," I whispered with relief and leaned on her again as we went out of the bathroom.

My three designated bodyguards were indeed waiting right in front of the door, their gazes filled with a mixture of concern and suspicion. It no doubt had little to do with my actual wellbeing, and only how it related to their jobs and probably their heads if anything went wrong with me. One of them was on the phone in a corner looking gloomy.

Now my heart thundered in my chest, hoping he wasn't speaking to Levan.

She took me back to my bed.

I immediately laid down and balled up into a fetal position as if in great pain.

A few moments later, she returned with a wheelchair and told them about the test she wanted to take me up for. "Just wait here," she said. "It's down the hall. We'll be back soon."

I was keeping my face turned away, so I couldn't gauge their reactions.

Then one of them interjected, "At least one of us has to come with her. No negotiations."

I had never heard him speak before, but I could guess who it was from the three, the burly guard with the shaved head and a horrid looking scar, running from his left eye in a mangled pattern, all the way to the back of his head. The thought of the pain and severity of whatever attack could have caused such an injury made me shiver when I first saw it.

With a sigh, she continued on her way.

My stomach was tied up in knots, but I couldn't lift my head or say a word as he followed us.

His face remained unsmiling and wary.

Soon, we got into a room full of equipment and she stopped just inside the doorway. "She has to change first," she said to him and shut the door solidly in his face. She moved me out of sight of the door's little glass window.

I instantly jumped up. "What are we going to do?"

"I'll handle this," she said firmly, pulling her phone out of her pocket. She called someone I assumed was a co-worker, and said, "Dede, can you come to the CBC lab? There's a man outside in a suit. Tell him that the doctor wants to see him concerning his ward ..." She looked at me enquiringly.

"Bianca Russet," I supplied.

"Bianca Russet," she said into the phone.

Whoever was on the phone with her must have asked her what the hell was going on, because she smiled, and told her," I'll explain later."

"Please tell her to hurry," I urged.

"And hurry up," she added and ended the call.

"What's your name?" I asked.

"Marjorie. Marjorie Dale."

"I'm going to find a way to pay you back, Marjorie."

"No need." She smiled. "Just go help that friend of yours."

Just then, my phone began to ring, startling the life out of me. I looked down to the caller ID and almost passed out when I saw who it was.

I muted my phone, but stared at the number until it disappeared. Almost immediately, it began ringing again and I knew he wouldn't stop until he spoke to me. I raised my gaze to see the look of concern in hers.

"Everything alright?" she asked.

"Yeah," I said, my voice strained. "But I need to get out of here A.S.A.P."

As if on cue the door opened and a pretty, petite nurse walked in with a curious look on her face. She had a mass of dark curls on her head and large hazel eyes.

"I'll tell you everything later," Marjorie said before she could say anything. She walked quickly to the glass window and waited a few seconds before she opened the door and looked out into the corridor.

Once she had ascertained that the coast was clear, I found myself being led through the door and down the emergency flight of stairs towards the back exit of the hospital.

I jumped down from the SUV and ran into the emergency room.

Immediately, I sighted Sergei.

He looked big and vital in that place full of fear and illness. He hurried over.

I stopped for a moment to catch my breath, my heart was pounding furiously in my chest.

"Where is she?" I asked.

There was a strange expression on Sergei's face.

"Where the fuck is she?" I demanded frantically.

He took a step back, and my eyes narrowed ... fear roiling in the pit of my stomach. A strange cold fog was invading my brain. Even the thought of her being hurt was impossible to hold in my head. My voice felt strange, distant, desperate as I asked, "Is she okay?"

"We hope so." Sergei said.

"What the fuck is that supposed to mean?"

"She gave us the slip, Boss," he finally admitted, "and we don't know where to."

My legs almost gave out. I knew what she was going to do.

I turned away from them and strode off towards the exit of the emergency ward.

They followed after me like lambs.

Bastards. The moment we reached outside, I *lost* it. The frustration and rage boiled over as I spun around and drove my fist into the first jaw it could connect with.

Yuri caught it and collapsed to the ground.

The others immediately stepped backwards.

A collective gasp rose up from the startled audience of paramedics and patients gathered in the surrounding area.

My face was throbbing, my ribs felt as if they were on fire, and my fist felt as if it had just hit a brick wall, but none of that mattered. "Tell me what happened," I ordered quietly calming myself, turning my attention to Orlaf.

"She was taken for a test, and then the nurse came out of the room and said that she had no idea where she had gone to, and that she had just disappeared. We tried immediately to find her, but she was long gone. I believe the nurse was in on it."

"What?"

They looked at me, and then at themselves as no more information seemed to be available.

"You said she was the one who called the ambulance right?"

"Yes sir," he replied.

"And they couldn't detect what was wrong with her even after she arrived at the hospital?"

"She couldn't speak, so the doctor couldn't help her."

"Hmm." I pulled out my phone and called her number, but she had either switched it off or her battery had died. I was guessing it was the former.

If he got a hold of her, it was over. He would hurt her in a way that she would never be able to recover from. Horrible pain *struck* me at the possibility ... I couldn't breathe.

I tried once again to reach her and when the message that her phone had been turned off was repeated to me, I stopped trying. I paused and thought hard about this.

Obviously, Bogdan didn't have her yet or he would have called to gloat.

Why did she run though?

She would only have put herself in danger if she was threatened or wanted to do something to save her father or ... I thought back to the house and recalled the open door to my study ... the video on the computer.

Damn! I dialed Alex.

"Put the girl on the phone," I said.

"Yes, Boss."

"Hey, Levan," Aldie answered a few seconds later.

"Did Bianca try to reach you?"

"I wouldn't know. I don't have any idea where my phone is."

"Fuck," I swore under my breath.

I ended the call and called Maxim. "I need to know where Bogdan is right now. I think ... Bianca saw the video in the study and might be going to him to save her friend."

"I don't know where he is," he said coldly. "If I knew then why the fuck would I have gone to the mart?"

"Then how did you know her friend was there?"

"I didn't. Bogdan was spotted there but he took off before we got there. We missed him and now, no one knows where he has crawled into. Until he pokes his miserable head out again his whereabouts are anybody's guess."

"I need to find him," I snarled.

"Forget about him," he said. "We have bigger problems. The Solicitor General's office just announced an emergency news conference in forty-five minutes. So you need to make a decision, right now. I'm giving you that courtesy at least. Who am I going to take out?"

I couldn't say a word.

At my silence, he went on, "Either Sarah Dale is silenced before that conference, or I contact Bogdan and offer the girl up on a platter."

I remained silent because he knew my answer.

He ended the call.

I thought of how to reach Bogdan.

My dad would probably know, but he had conveniently disappeared. The only other person who could reach Bogdan ...I couldn't speak to.

My chest ached at the thought of the man I was walking away from. My eyes stung and filled with tears, but I blinked them away furiously. This was neither the time nor the place.

Currently, I sat outside the 7-Eleven I had managed to walk to. I thought hard on what to do, my nerves sizzling at the thought of how Aldie was losing time. What if Levan had found her?

My heart skipped at the possibility. I looked at my dead phone, then glimpsed for the umpteenth time into the convenience store.

I rose to my feet and made my way into the store.

I didn't have a single dime on me, so my only hope was the cashier would overlook my lack of a purchase and help me.

The man behind the counter had ginger hair and comically large ears. He was munching quite loudly on a bag of chips as he watched the news on the small television by his side.

I approached him with a massive smile on my face.

His eyes narrowed at my suspiciously positive approach. He sent me a tight-lipped smile in response and went back to his news until I reached him.

"Hi," I said. "I'm Bianca and I um ... I have a huge favor to ask of you."

"Look, I'm just the cashier, so I'm not authorized to give *anybody* store credit. The manager won't get here until this evening, and there's a surveillance camera up there watching you," he said in a bored tone, his gaze still on the news.

I brought out my phone. "Can I borrow your charger for just a few minutes? It's an emergency and I need to call someone to come pick me up."

He looked from me, to my dead phone, and back to me. "I don't use that. I have an iPhone."

I looked at the Samsung in my hands and I was about to ask to borrow his phone when the news coming from his TV grabbed my attention.

There was a room of reporters and cameras and the breaking headlines underneath read:

*Former attorney general of New York to reveal
shady dealings with Russian conglomerate!*

THE REPORTER WENT on to explain that Sarah Dale, called for the meeting an hour earlier, to answer a claim that she had been in bed with the Ivankov conglomerate and how the company had through this tie, avoided prosecution from the authorities.

My heart dropped into my stomach. Now things were beginning to fall in place. I turned away from the TV screen. "I need to borrow your phone extremely urgently please," I said, my eyes no doubt filled with panic, but I tried to keep my voice even.

The redhead turned to me with a scowl. "Look," he began sternly.

I didn't let him continue, "Please, *please,*" I begged. "I need to contact someone immediately. It's a matter of life and death. I promise you'll be saving someone's life."

With a long-suffering sigh, he unlocked his device and passed it over.

I took the phone gratefully. "Thank you so much."

He stared at me curiously. "Go on then. Make that life and death call of yours."

The only person's phone number I had off the top of my head was Aldie's and my dad's. Levan's I had no clue of, and definitely not Bogdan's. The frustration was all-encompassing. I looked at him. "I might have to make two calls, but they are both very important."

Before he could say anything, I quickly dialed Aldie's number. I don't know what I expected, but I felt pain when I reached her dead number. I glanced up at the redhead.

He still sat, looking at me with a disappointed expression.

"Just one more number," I said and dialed my father's number. To my shock, it rang. For the first time since he had last sold me off, his phone was on.

I waited, digging my nails into my palm and praying to every God there was, that he would pick up.

He did, his voice extremely cautious as he said, "Hello."

"Dad?"

"Bee?" he asked surprised. The relief in his voice was colossal.

"Dad," I called. "Where are you?"

"I—uh ... I-I can't tell you that right now, baby, I'm so sorry. Actually, I can't even stay on the phone long. I just switched it on to get a contact."

I was suddenly filled with crippling disappointment and fury towards this man and all the damage he had caused me. Everyone else other than him was fighting for me. I looked at the television and saw the one person who didn't owe me anything in the world about to be ruined, and all because of me. I was certain that somehow, Bogdan had contributed to this.

"I want Bogdan's phone number," I said sadly.

"What?"

"Don't ask me any questions. Just send it to me. Right now!"

"You're not with him? What's going on?"

"Just please send it! He's about to fucking kill Aldie!" My voice ended on a sob.

I never cursed, especially not at him, so at the rage ... he immediately complied. "Alright."

I ended the call, took a deep breath, then I turned towards the boy.

His eyes were as huge as saucers now.

"Just one more call," I said.

He nodded speechlessly.

His phone pinged and I handed it to him so he could retrieve Bogdan's phone number for me.

A few seconds later and I was on the call to the beast.

He answered in Russian aggressively, and impatiently.

"Bogdan, this is Bianca," I said expressionlessly. "Come pick me up. And if you lay your hands in anyway on my best friend I will find a way to kill you myself.

29

LEVAN

I sat alone in the car park of the hospital, my head resting on the steering wheel. Soon, it would be dawn.

I had needed the time to think, to resolve the current dilemma that my life was about to shatter and crumble beneath me.

A sob choked my throat as I thought of her. Bogdan couldn't get to her before I did ... he just couldn't. He fucking couldn't. I couldn't allow it. I felt as if I'd been stripped of everything. Nothing mattered anymore except finding her, saving her.

I pounded on the steering wheel in fury.

It startled the men who were waiting outside. One of them walked up to the car window.

I didn't bother rolling down the window or acknowledging him. With a flick of my hand, I waved him away and turned to pick up my phone to call Maxim. He would know what to do ... he had to. I wasn't equipped to deal with psychopaths like Bogdan. My first instinct was to play fair, but Maxim had been dealing with men like Bogdan from the time he was seventeen.

He picked up on the second ring.

"Maxim," I said, and my voice sounded distraught and inconsolable. "I need to find her before he does. If he does, I won't be okay. I won't be able to move past this."

He was silent for a while.

"Please, Max. I'll owe you big time. I'll do anything."

"I'll find her ..." he said and ended the call.

I was about to fling the phone to the passenger seat when it began to ring again and at the sight of the caller, my blood froze over.

His deep, grating laughter filled the air ... boisterous and glad, and for the first time — it filled me with fear.

"My Prince. You will never guess the gift I have just received."

I felt my heart collapse. My free hand fisted and swung, striking the window so hard, my wrist popped, and the glass cracked.

One of the men rushed up to me and I pointed at the phone. He nodded in agreement and immediately hastened to contact headquarters.

I needed to keep him on the line.

Somehow, I got my mouth to move. "Where is she? Can I

speak to her?" There was no need for him to allow me to speak to her, but I knew he wouldn't be able to resist the urge to gloat. '

"She's safe with my men. Hold on and one of them will call you." His voice boomed triumphantly and the call ended suddenly.

A few moments later, my phone rang, and I heard her voice.

"Levan?" She sounded small and frightened.

"Have they hurt you?"

"No," she replied.

"Okay, just stay on the line with me for a while ..." I said to her.

"Levan, I saw that ..."

"Don't say a word," I urged. "Just know, everything is going to be fine."

Before she could answer the phone was torn from her hold and the call went dead. I hardened my heart and waited. I knew he couldn't resist one last gloat. My phone rang and I was back with Bogdan.

"Thanks for this gift, my Prince ... oh, and about the press conference ... it's too late to halt that now. Moreover, that bitch needs to work to get her grandson back just as we all have to, to get what we want." He ended the call with a laugh.

I immediately looked to the guys beyond the windshield, my gaze widened with the question.

Yuri was listening in on the call. Soon, he put the phone away and came up to me. "They couldn't track her, boss, the call ended too quickly."

I went still and he knew to walk away. It felt as though the life had been zapped out of me.

I looked ahead but saw absolutely nothing. My phone began to ring again and I picked it up.

It was Maxim. "Levan," he said. "She's on Levison Avenue, South River. I'll send you the full address."

I started the engine. "I'm heading over there right now." I didn't think at all, I just put the vehicle into motion and zoomed off into the darkness. In the rearview mirror, I could see my men throwing their hands up in confusion but I knew they would soon track me.

I BEAT every traffic light I came across and thirty minutes later, I was approaching the cul-de-sac of an average income neighborhood, when I received another call from Maxim.

"Is there a problem?" I asked. "Has he moved from there?"

"Have you lost your fucking mind, Levan?" His voice snapped over the phone. "You left without backup."

"I'll be fine."

"You've truly lost it if you think you'll be fine walking into Bogdan's turf with nothing but your rage to steal back something he's shown he's prepared to fight to the death to keep." He cut the call.

I knew he was right. However, now it was too late for after-thoughts. I was here and kept on going past the address. A few houses down, I cut the engine and made a quick call to Maxim. "How close are your guys?"

"Luckily for you, five minutes away," he said crisply.

"I'll survey the surroundings. Get here fast and quietly."

"Yes, of course."

Bogdan's temporary hiding hole was in a modest, split-level house. The same as a simple family of four would be living in, the same as the entire uneventful neighborhood for that matter.

The perfect camouflage.

No movement could be detected in the house. There were a few lights on inside, but nothing could be seen from where I stood with the shrubbery that lined the property. I nearly held my breath as my whole body was throbbing with impatience to go in.

Suddenly, there was movement.

The door opened as a couple of men and a woman I would recognize anywhere, came out. They were on the move.

I unholstered my gun and cocked it.

30

"Where are we going?" I asked for the umpteenth time, but there was no response.

I stopped for a moment, but was pushed from behind. I wasn't expecting it and I stumbled onto the stone driveway.

One of them stopped and knelt beside me. "Get up bitch! You show us up here and that little friend of yours gets a bullet in her head, but not before all of us gang rape her," he growled softly.

Goosebumps erupted all over my flesh. I jumped to my feet, but decided to make my stand here. It was a modest, quiet neighborhood and it was my best bet to get anywhere with these men. A boy cycled past. "You have me now. Just let my friend go. I'm not going anywhere with you if you don't let her go first."

One of the men laughed.

"We'll let her go when we please but first, you have a lot of apologies to make to the boss."

"You'll be doing most of that on your hands and knees," the man who laughed said.

Glancing around, I saw a neighbor's curtains twitch. It gave me courage. "I'm not going anywhere until I know she has been set free," I insisted stubbornly.

One of them grabbed my hair then, my neck tilted in an excruciating angle. "You ever been fucked upside down, cupcake?"

The curtain on the neighbor's window fell back down. Whoever it was either didn't want to get involved, or had gone to call the police. Either way, it wouldn't help me any.

I tried to break away from the painful hold on my scalp, but he wouldn't budge. Then just as suddenly, he let go and I fell to the ground, my elbows landing painfully on the asphalt. Tears threatened, but I steeled my stomach and found my way once again to my feet. The men grabbed me again.

A car pulled up then, and the driver rushed down from the driver's seat to pull the door open for me to enter. Inside, Bogdan was waiting for me. He barked something at the men holding me in Russian and they let go of me. I looked at the men and wished with all my heart that I could just do something that would magically set Aldie and myself free. But it was all wishful thinking. What was I, a young woman, untrained in this brutal world going to do against these cruel men? In a panic, I had left the security of Levan's home and ended up here, still no closer to saving Aldie.

I swallowed hard the turmoil that was making waves in my stomach and looked into the car at the smug, ugly face of Bogdan and I knew it was going to be him or me. I would rather die than prostitute myself to him. The first chance I got, after I knew Aldie was safe, I was going to end his life. One way or another. And this time, I wouldn't be trying to use a butter knife.

I took a step towards the car ... and the sound of a gunshot almost *blasted* my ear off. I screamed and found myself crashing to the ground. I was sure I had been hit. Then after a few seconds amidst the roars and commotion around me, I opened my eyes and met the open, now soulless eyes of the man who had been standing behind me. He had been shot through the side of his head, and dark red blood was pooling around him on the sidewalk.

I scrambled away in terror, too shocked to run. There was another gunshot seemingly right by my side and I screamed in pure fear. I turned to see that it had been aimed at the tire beside me. Answering gunshots were fired from Bogdan's men. All I wanted to do was to crawl under the car where there might be some safety.

Suddenly, the car started and I heard orders being roared in Russian. Before I could comprehend much, I was pulled up to my feet so roughly it felt as if my arm had been torn out of its socket.

I cried out in pain, then I was thrown into the vehicle like a rag doll. The door had barely been shut closed when the vehicle with three tires screeched away from the pavement. We drove madly through the street as I tried to catch my breath.

I didn't want to look to see what was going on as the car careened down the road at as much speed as it could with one shot-out tire. Burying my head in my arms, I couldn't help the scream that tore out of my mouth when another gunshot pierced through the window and glass shattered all over me. The car swerved so hard I was flung across the seat. Terrified, I tried to find something to hold onto. My hand found the seatbelt and I managed to fasten it just as the car left the ground.

Oh God, we were flying. Straight towards a lamppost.

The sound of the car crashing into the post was horrible. Metal crunched and moved inwards crushing the driver.

I screamed with terror.

Then everything went quiet. I didn't even dare look to my left, where Bogdan had been sitting.

https://www.youtube.com/watch?v=wtT3qs96ybo

B lood was running down my head into one eye.

I rubbed it away and tried to see through the haze of smoke. Unlatching my seat belt, I dragged myself out of the car. I had crashed into Bogdan's car when I saw an oncoming white van that would narrowly miss them and crash into me, which would mean Bogdan would escape. In that insane split-second, it felt as if everything slowed down and my senses became super-sharp. I felt as if I had 360-degree vision. Everything became crystal clear. I could even feel my clothes brush against my skin, blood seep down my face, the trickle of sweat roll down my spine, the air that I breathed, the grain on the leather of the steering wheel, the fire in my ribcage, the throbbing in my swollen nose, but the only thing that mattered was saving Bianca Russet.

My instinct became so keen I didn't have to calculate where in his car she was sitting. I knew exactly where to ram. My heart seized at the thought that she would get thrown forward, but my brain calculated that the size of the driver in front of her would probably mean if she was thrown forward, she would slam into him and not go through the windshield. It was either that or the risk of Bogdan getting away with her.

It would have been game over then.

So I slammed into Bogdan's car. So hard, I launched it into the air. The on-coming van sped past. I even saw the driver's shocked expression.

My leg felt like it had been crushed, but I staggered out. Gun in hand as I was about to move towards the somersaulted vehicle by the side of the road when there was the screech of an approaching vehicle. I hoped it was Maxim's men or my guys, but cautiously I crouched down. The moment I noticed that they were Bogdan's guys, I aimed my gun at them, ready for the moment when they tried to retrieve Bianca from the crash.

They hurried over to the car and looked into the driver's window.

What they saw there made them rush over to the side where Bogdan was. They couldn't pry the door open, but they were large strong men and they made the job of pulling their unconscious boss out of the car window look like child's play. They carried his body to their SUV and laid him inside.

Then they turned back and started towards the wreckage

again. That was the moment I fired my first shot. I didn't want to hit either of them, it was just a little incentive for them to get out of there with their boss, but when they began firing back at me, my stomach twisted in fury.

One of their fucking bullets was going to hit Bianca.

I took aim and was about to drop one of them when we all heard the screech of approaching vehicles.

Bogdan's men didn't need further incentives to leave. They jumped into their SUV and escaped with their boss as they sped their way down the dark empty road.

I limped over as quickly as I could towards the smoking wreckage. I looked in through the shattered window of the vehicle and found her figure twisted and unconscious.

My heart lurched into my throat and I lost it.

I flung my gun to the ground then kicked and fought with the mangled door like a mad man until my guys came around to help me.

They had metal cutting instruments with them and they pried the door open.

With bleeding fingers, I reached in to get to my girl. Carefully, I extricated her from the safety belt that had held her in place and took her into my arms.

Pushing her hair out of her face, I pressed my finger to her pulse. The beat of her blood, although faint, was steady. The blood from my head dropped to her face and with tears in my eyes, I wiped it off. I sat with her unconscious body on the ground and rocked her, unable to move, or let go.

I had lost my mind. I had completely and utterly lost my mind over this troublesome, disobedient, beautiful woman.

As if it came from far away, I heard myself speak, "Get us home now."

Then blackness descended on me. I tried to fight it desperately, to not give in to it. I wanted to stay and protect Bianca, but it swept me away.

32

BIANCA

I came awake, and for the first few moments, my brain couldn't understand where I was, but as the decor and fittings around the room began to register, I realized I was back in Levan's home.

This was his room.

But I couldn't be here. If I were then it meant that ... *Aldie.*

I bolted upright to a sitting position and almost doubled over by the jarring pain from bruises all over my body. A violent headache started up in my head. The pain threatened to split it into two, but I wouldn't back down. With my hand pressed to my head, I ran to the door and pulled it open. I went down the corridor and as I reached the top of the staircase, I saw a figure arrive at the bottom of the stairs.

She was holding a tray of juice. She looked up when she noticed my presence.

I couldn't move. "Aldie?" I whispered, almost in disbelief.

She put the tray down on a little side-table and ran lightly up the stairs to me. There were tears in her eyes. "Why are you up? You need to rest."

I drew her into my arms and held her close. I inhaled her warm, lovely scent as I molded myself into her familiar contours and thanked God. Tears rolled uncontrollably from my eyes. "Aldie," I sobbed. "I'm so sorry."

She pulled away from me, her eyes gentle. "Hey, hey, hey, don't apologize. You have nothing to apologize for. It was not your fault."

"I saw what they did to you!" I cried, inconsolable that because of me she had suffered pain at the hands of those brutes. My eyes searched her face and body for signs that she had suffered damage. "Are you sure you're alright?"

She nodded and opened her arms out. "Look at me. I'm fine. A few bruises. Other than that, I'm as good as new."

"I'm really sorry."

"Stop freaking apologizing," she said sternly.

I shook my head in wonder. "How did you get here?"

"Levan came to get me. You didn't need to give yourself up to Bogdan at all."

"What?" I asked my head spinning at that information. If only I'd waited a little longer, I cursed inside. My body swayed with shock.

Aldie quickly caught my hand to lead me back to my room. "Why don't you go back to sleep for a bit and I'll explain everything when you wake up."

"What about Levan?" I asked. "Is he okay?"

She took me into the room and sat me down on the couch.

And then she explained it all.

"What?" I gazed at Aldie, my heart in my throat. "He's wanted?"

"Yeah," she said solemnly. "The warrant was issued after the press conference four hours ago. Sarah revealed everything about her dealings with Levan over the last two years. The allegations and people involved are just unbelievable. It's all gone national too."

"Where is he now?"

"I don't know. After dropping you off and making sure that you were okay, he left the house again. Perhaps he's off to do damage control."

"For which disaster?" I muttered, placing my hands on my head, and hiding my face between my knees. "I'm destroying him, Aldie. All of this is because of me, and seeing his whole world go down in flames is killing me." Every word that came out of my mouth rang through my heart as I came to realize just what this man, who was giving up so much for me ... meant to me.

However the debts he'd racked up along the way ... the deaths ... half of the country's law enforcement was about to be after him ... neither of us could pay. "I need to somehow put an end to this, Aldie."

She pulled me into her arms. "Come on, Bianca. There is

not a thing you can do. Just stop worrying, babe. It will all be fine."

"I don't believe that." I shook my head. "I don't believe that at all. Especially as Bogdan was able to get away. He's going to come back, Aldie, and he's going to come back for blood. I need your phone."

"Bee."

I went past her to head down the stairs.

"Bianca!" She called after me. "Bianca!

We arrived at the bottom of the stairs.

Just then, the front door was pushed open.

Maxim came in and ... we both froze.

Levan was behind him.

The sight of Levan made my whole body hurt all over.

He looked battered; his eyes bloodshot, his nose bruised into a sickly shade of purple. A bandage was wrapped around his head, and his shirt which was once crisp, was now raggedly and stained with dirt and blood.

Maxim gave a hard look at me. "Get her back to bed," he said sternly to Aldie, and went on his way down the hall.

To my surprise, Levan came up to me as he looked into my eyes. "Go with Aldie, Bianca. Rest. I have much to do now, but we'll talk later, okay?"

I wanted to protest. I wanted to hold him, but I knew from

his eyes, things were really serious and the best thing I could do to help was stay out of his way. I nodded.

He kissed me gently on the nose and walked in the same direction his brother had gone.

"His brother ..." Aldie said. "Is fucking frightening."

As we were turning away, there was a sudden commotion outside with sirens and shouts.

"What the fuck?" Aldie muttered as my gaze flew towards the door.

The deafening ruckus got closer.

Levan and Maxim rushed out, as the door burst open and four police officers came in with deadly expressions on their faces and guns in their grip. They pointed it at Levan, and surrounded him like a vicious pack of hyenas. "Put your hands above your head," they ordered.

"Levan!" I cried in fear.

He looked at me and smiled, then he put his hands into the air.

One of the police officers stepped forward, pulled his hands roughly down, and placed the handcuffs around his wrists. "Levan Ivankov," the officer said. "You have the right to remain silent. If you do say anything, what you say can be used against you in a court of law. You have the right to consult with a lawyer and have that lawyer present during any questioning. If you cannot afford a lawyer, one will be appointed for you if you so desire."

A few more officers charged in.

As they lead him away, he looked into my eyes. *"Stay here and wait for me,"* he mouthed.

Then he was gone.

I turned my shocked gaze to Maxim.

When he felt my gaze, he turned to look at me. His eyes were hostile. It was clear he blamed me. Then he turned around and went back the way he had come.

I felt my legs give out and I collapsed to the floor. I shook so hard that my body was vibrating.

Aldie crouched down next to me and pulled me into her arms.

I felt cold. Very, very cold.

33

Five million dollars and six hours later, I was bailed out of jail. I walked out of the station to see Maxim leaning against a waiting SUV.

I stopped and watched him.

And he did the same to me. "Your head clear yet?" he asked.

I knew he was pissed about the huge bail, so I gave him a hard look and went around to the door Alex held open. He nodded in greeting but I barely even noticed him. Maxim got in and we began our journey back to the house.

We both remained quiet until we arrived. The moment the engine was cut off, Maxim turned to me. "You're not going to apologize for thinking with your dick?"

"I took a calculated risk," I said. "And I'll do everything in my power to ensure that it doesn't sink us, but I'm not giving up Bianca."

He scowled. "Is that your apology?"

"What do you want me to fucking say?" I snapped.

The two men in front immediately jumped out of the car.

"I've told you from the very beginning," I went on. "That I didn't want to get involved in the family business. This is your thing, not mine. I'm not cut out for this life. But then I didn't have much of a choice, did I? She is the one choice I will not allow anyone else to make for me. I'm not going to say it again. I'm not going to abandon her, no matter what."

He looked away from me in thought. "Dad's out for blood and is furious about this situation. He wants you in Spain before the end of the week."

"I'm not allowed to leave the country."

"It's not a *request*. You can go ahead and make another *choice* if you so desire, but don't forget attending funerals of loved ones is also a choice in our family." He got out and slammed the car door behind him.

This left me alone in the car, cold and breathless with fury all over again. Despite the hand my father had in my mother's death, he had chosen to attend a gathering of ministers in Tokyo rather than attend her funeral.

The warning from Maxim was directed towards Bianca. It had been noted. My father was a stone-cold man. Nothing stood in the way of his goal. Sometimes, I thought even Maxim and me could be sacrificed at the altar of his ambition. Definitely, Bianca would stand no chance.

I got out of the car and quickly walked to the house. When I came inside, I noted Aldie by the doorway to the kitchen.

She was waiting, her gaze filled with anxiety, but she hesitated in coming forward to meet me.

I nodded at her then walked up the stairs to my room and shut the door.

34

BIANCA

I was lying in bed, my eyes wide open and staring at the ceiling. I hadn't slept a wink and it had absolutely nothing to do with the rain outside, pouring heavily down.

With a sigh, I turned my head to watch the downpour beyond my window.

I loved the rain, but it wasn't Levan's favorite thing. My mind went back to a day two years ago. I had been working late in the bakery when a sudden knock on the glass door of our store had startled me and made me jump.

I'd spun around to see Levan by the door, soaking wet, a big smile on his face.

On his way in, he tripped, and almost landed on his butt on the floor if not for some fancy footwork. With a laugh neither of us could control, I'd asked him what he was doing across the Brooklyn Bridge at 3.00 a.m. It didn't matter what he would have said anyway, my heart felt as if it was melting at the mere sight of him. I couldn't believe it, especially as it brought the stirrings of hope that perhaps he was beginning to see me as more than an acquaintance if nothing else.

"I was craving your bacon cupcake," he said, with a wolfish grin.

I grinned back. "You came all the way from East Village for a cupcake?"

"I couldn't sleep. They were all I could think about."

The way he said the words had made me reach out to hold onto something. My hands had connected with the hard edge of the wooden table. Cringing with embarrassment, I'd walked away to hide just how smitten I was with him. "We're actually closed," I said.

He'd come over to lean against the counter to watch me.

"Shall I get you a towel?" I asked awkwardly.

"Nope."

I cleared my throat. "Like I said, we're ... um ... kind of closed."

"I know, but Aldie mentioned you took requests from people you liked."

I lowered my head to hide my smile. "And you would qualify?"

"I'm hoping that I do."

I'd taken another deep shaky breath again and returned to the dough I had been rolling. When I trusted my voice to remain stable, I replied, "We don't have any more of those. We're sold out of them."

He came around the counter.

At his approach, my heart stopped.

"Let's make some together." Even though he was supposedly talking about bacon cupcakes, his voice, and eyes told me a different story.

I began to back away as though I was being cornered.

"Maybe you can teach me," he said softly.

"Um ... you're not supposed to be back here."

He immediately stopped then, hands in the air, his beautiful eyes almost slate gray with some emotion I didn't understand.

His very presence was scrambling my brain.

"I'll leave, but I'm not going without my cupcakes. You can name your price. I'm that desperate for a taste."

I had stared at him, lost with my heart beating so hard my chest ached. Did he feel the same way I did? Someone as gorgeous as him? "Uh?"

He'd looked back at the rain pouring through the glass doors and turned back to me with a soft, desperate look. "I hate the rain ... please don't make me go back out there."

That day felt so far away now. We were both so young and I was so full of hope for the future. Today, I felt as though something blunt and rusty had been stabbed into my stomach. I turned away from the window and my gaze went back to the ceiling. Did he actually hate the rain or had he just said that to ensure that I didn't throw him out? And in the same vein, I'd never been able to ascertain for sure how he felt about me. Some days back then, he couldn't take his eyes off me, then he walked away without a word.

I rose up from the bed and found myself walking to his room. He was not in, but I just wanted to lie on his bed again, breathe in his scent.

I knocked on his door just as a courtesy, in case one of the maids was in there, but before I could even retract my hand, the door was pulled open suddenly.

It was almost so unexpected I nearly fell into him.

Levan reached out for me, firm hands on my arms, and when he seemed sure I was steady again, he let me go.

I felt the loss so keenly.

He stared into my eyes, his expression remaining unreadable.

My mind spun. He was back and he did not even bother to come to me. "I— um ..."

His jaw was covered in dark stubble, his nose still badly bruised and swollen, the wound on his forehead protected by a bandage. It pained me severely to see him so battered, but I also lost my ability to breathe from how relieved I was to see him alive and so close to me. All I could think of was grazing my finger across his beard ... tasting his sweet hot mouth and having his cock fill the throb of emptiness in my core. I couldn't even remember why I had come here.

I looked over his shoulder to see the pelting rain coursing down the massive windows, and I remembered. "I wanted to ask you a question."

He raised an eyebrow as if to say go on, then winced, when the simple action hurt him.

"Do you ... um really not like the rain?"

He shook his head. "What?'

"Remember that early morning when you came to the bakery looking for bacon cupcakes," I explained, "you said you hated the rain."

His eyes fluttered shut for a brief tender moment.

I found mine filling with tears. "I'm sorry, Levan."

He opened his eyes. "For what?"

I bit my bottom lip. "I'm so sorry for putting you into this mess. I'm sorry for making your brother angry with you, for the loss I am causing your family financially, and for the legal troubles I've brought to you."

"Hmm ... why don't you come in, Bianca." He stepped back.

I accepted the quiet invite and walked in. Shutting the door behind me I watched as he walked away toward his bathroom.

"I was just about to wash when you knocked. Will you wait for me? I won't be long."

"No problem," I said quickly.

And he disappeared into his bathroom.

I stopped for a moment to think of whether I would be too overbearing if I followed him. I'd been too worried, felt too guilty, too scared and terrified of never seeing him again to care if he thought me too overbearing. I just needed to be near him. My bare feet were soundless as I headed into his bathroom. Inside the marble space, I saw that he was already in the massive shower stall.

Through the frosted glass, I could see his lithe, silhouette under the cascade of hot steaming water. His body was made for the kind of *fucking* that I had enjoyed only with him ... raw, primal, possessive and utterly addictive.

Unbridled lust soaked my underwear as I watched him, the anxiety at even being here given the tension brimming around us, and the vividly clear memories of exactly what his mouth and cock could do to me set my blood ablaze. I definitely could not, and would not leave. I still held one more card and I was certain it would be more than enough to shatter the distance that had sprung up between us.

I pulled off my night shorts, underwear, and then pulled my t-shirt over my head. Letting it all fall to the floor. When I arrived at the glass door, I pulled it open without hesitation.

He turned then, sweeping the water out of his face, his eyes roving over my naked body.

The look in his eyes made my heart pound like crazy. Before he could say anything, I stepped into the stall. "I'm sorry I didn't trust you. I'm sorry I went to Bogdan, Levan," I whispered. "I know I've caused you much pain in the last week and the last thing I want to do is cause you more trouble, but once I saw the video of Aldie being slapped around by those brutes, I lost my head. I couldn't let her suffer for me. She doesn't deserve that. She's always been the one light in my depressing life. Please understand I had to help her no matter what. I love her like she is my own flesh and blood. I never expected that any of this would happen."

"It's okay," he said softly.

He was so forgiving my heart broke a little. "I feel really guilty and horrible. You went to jail for God's sake, and I'm so terrified of what is going to happen to you. I'm afraid you'll end up in prison and start to hate me," I said on a sob.

He reached out a hand. "I'll never hate you, Bianca."

My eyes filled with tears. "Are — are you going to prison?"

He shrugged. "Maybe. I haven't heard the charges Sarah has made, but it'll be hard to walk away from this without doing time."

"Two years ago, why did you leave without a word? Was it because of the message I sent to you? You saw it and decided I was too desperate for you."

"I told you ..."

"I know you got shot, but what about afterwards? What about after you healed?"

"You were the most perfect human being I had ever met and I didn't want you involved in my violent world, Bianca."

I understood the context of his words, especially now more than ever, but it still hurt. All those years of thinking he'd just walked away from me. I bit my lip. "Wasn't that choice mine to make?"

He shook his head. "No. It was my duty to protect you from danger. Getting shot made me realize more than ever the danger I would be putting you constantly in. The life that I would be forcing you to live. I couldn't do that to you."

"But that was my decision to make," I insisted.

He looked at me sadly. "I watched my mom constantly look over her shoulder, in fear for her life. I watched her wither away in constant worry for the lives of her husband and children. Is that what you would have wanted?"

I want you and I don't give a damn if I get killed in the process, I wanted to scream back at him, but I didn't have the courage to say it out loud to either him, or for that matter, myself.

When I didn't answer, he slid the door of the stall open to step out, but I slid it back shut, and forced him to face me. "Why exactly are you helping me, Levan? Is it just to ensure I'm safe, before you toss me back into the world, or are you planning to keep me for yourself?"

To my surprise, he placed his hands on the sides of my face. I melted into his touch.

He pulled me to him, my naked body settling into the hard planes of his. "I'm so sorry, Bianca. How can I promise you anything, when I could end up in prison for the rest of my life?"

"What are you saying?" I asked, almost too afraid to speak. "So your plan is to toss me back into the world?"

When he remained silent, I lifted my head and looked into his eyes.

Eventually he spoke, his voice full of anguish, "What can I do, Bianca? Tell me how I can keep you?" His eyes roamed over my face, searching.

I wasn't sure what he was searching for and maybe, I didn't want to know. I lifted myself on the tips of my toes, and slipped my tongue into his mouth. I kissed him at first softly, then fervently as the desperation from wanting him more than I could now comprehend, overwhelmed me.

Something heavy hung in the air like a cry or warning for the both of us not to go any further, not to fall any deeper, but I pushed it away. It was a painful kiss and before I could tell whether the moisture I felt rolling down our cheeks was mine or his, he led me under the cascade of water with him.

As the water drummed on my head, I reached up to run my fingers through his hair. I wanted so much to believe that perhaps everything would be fine.

His arms went around my waist to glue me to his body as the fascinating hardness of his cock pressed against my stomach. The pulse of my sex, throbbing with an almost painful awareness of how much this man consumed me.

He traced wet, sweet kisses along my jaw, my gasp entangled with his breath as I hung onto his bulky arms for dear life.

I ran my fingers through his hair. "Does it still hurt?" I asked, my finger moving softly over the still bruised bridge of his nose.

"I'll live," he answered, tracing the curves of my hips as he kissed me, softly and then deeply. His hands moved upwards and settled tenderly on the sides of my throat as his lips pressed against my temple.

A jolt of pleasure stole my breath. I kissed him senseless.

Suddenly, my back was pressed against the tiled wall and his hands were digging greedily into my ass. He crushed me against his hardness making the ache that we felt for each other ring in our bones.

My head fell back against the wall in breathless anticipation as he got on his knees and his mouth covered my soaked and ready sex, my back arched. "Oh *fuck* ... *Levan*," I breathed, as I parted my thighs even further to make sure I did not accidentally hurt his swollen nose.

This intimacy between us was all that was needed to drive me wild. Shamelessly, I lifted a leg to give his tongue deeper access into my body. I felt every nerve in my body tighten with the most delicious torment as he speared into me, then greedily lapped up the juices that spilled out onto his tongue.

The hard suction of his lips on my clit, and the velvet dance of his tongue through the folds of my sex had me thrashing against the wall, almost unable to bear his thorough possession of me, but at the same time, I was certain I would lose my mind if he stopped.

I rode his tongue greedily ... chasing the release that was so close. All I could feel and sense was him, and it felt as though he were burning me deliciously alive. My eyes and mind shut to everything beyond what he was doing to me.

My climax came.

I quivered as the wonderful waves of pleasure overcame me, but even as I began to drown in bliss, I remained conscious of his injuries. I grabbed his hair and pulled his head away so that my jerking body would not hurt him. As the intense pleasure began to spiral out, I started to lose it. I felt my body start to sway as if I was a flower stalk in a strong wind.

Eventually, I was shaking so hard, even his fingers digging into the flesh of my thighs wasn't enough to keep me stable, and he had to press me against the wall. As the waves began to subside, I opened my eyes and looked down at him.

The water was falling on his face and his eyes looked beautiful beyond anything I'd seen before. I felt such love pour into my heart. I wanted to tell him I loved him then, but the words stuck in my throat when he shoved a finger, and then another, inside of me. I gasped as my hips restarted their rocking rhythm. I felt crazed and completely possessed by him.

His fingers plunged hard and fast inside me. I sought desperately for the reigns of some sort of stability or control, but I could tell that this time would not be like the last. Last time, I still remembered not to hurt him, but this time there was a possibility I would be completely lost. "Levan," I breathed his name out helplessly, as my orgasm built and approached like a raging storm, ready to destroy everything in its path. I feared for my sanity. I started to push him away once more, but his grip and hold on me was iron-clad.

His tongue alighted on my clit and I was gone.

When I found myself again, I was gasping and slamming my cunt like a crazed woman into his mouth. Thankfully, he hadn't lost his mind and knew to keep his nose clear of harm. "*Levan.*" I shuddered, quaking against him.

His magical tongue never let up. Then his mouth closed down on my whole sex, hard and hot.

I collapsed like a cheap chair. All the bones in my body melted. My hands stretched forward and curled with the excruciating need to grab onto something ... anything. I was near collapse. My fingers touched the wet shower rod and I quickly grasped it hard. Then ... all I could do was moan out the rapture of my release. "Ohhhhh, *fuck!*" My knees gave way and I could feel my body slipping down the tiles. He rose then and caught me. I hid my face in his chest as a sob choked me, and he lovingly held me while my orgasm tore through me.

"You're going to fucking kill me," I gasped when it was all over.

He pulled me away from his chest and kissed me hard. Water ran down our faces. It was sensuous and hot, but I wasn't ready to move yet, not after the fleet of orgasms that had just rocked me senseless.

I pulled away and stared into his eyes. My heart felt as if it would burst with the love I felt for him, again I wanted to tell him I loved him.

Just then, he grabbed his thick, hard cock and bending his knees, he settled the long, intimidating length between my folds. A breathless moan escaped my lips as he held it in place, and then began to rock his hips smoothly and sensually between my sensitive, engorged lips.

"Levan," I breathed, biting down on the junction between his neck and shoulders.

"You're driving me out of my mind, Bianca," he rasped out.

I lifted my eyes to meet the smoldering look in his. He was too hot, in a way that I couldn't understand nor comprehend. He lifted me up and my feet left the ground as his cock plunged into me.

"Fuuuck," I cried out at the sudden intrusion, my mouth frozen in a soundless O.

He gave a knowing smile.

"You're so evil," I told him.

Then I saw his eyes flutter close with pleasure as he savored the feel of himself inside of me.

The walls of my sex were tight around him ... greedy and possessive. We were the perfect fit.

"Fuck me, Levan," I breathed. I didn't need to ask twice.

He slammed his hips forward, then pummeled into me. The sound of his flesh smacking mine mingled with the sound of the water and echoed in that small space.

"If only you knew what you did to me," he grunted in my ear. "You fucking terrify me, Bianca. One of these days, you're going to make me lose my mind."

I was the one who was already completely gone. Never had I felt so consumed and possessed. I couldn't utter a word, or formulate a single thought beyond the torrent of pleasure rippling through me.

His rhythm quickened, and I almost couldn't keep up. I whimpered and actually cried out for help that I most definitely did not want or need.

Our bodies were wild and slamming into the other. I caught his lips and drank him in, and drowning wholly in him and all that he meant to me.

Our orgasm built violently, and rose in unison. It seemed feral and unstoppable, like a force that did not belong to us, but had been bestowed fleetingly on us. He shuddered against me. We touched the peak together. I screamed his name and I was sure I was wounding him everywhere, but I couldn't stop. I had never felt such exquisite bliss. In that moment ... we were one.

I couldn't breathe and he didn't stop his thrusting. Deep inside me, I felt the hot bursts of his release.

And then ... he *stilled*, to savor the sheer torrent of our unreal and magical climax. It felt as though his body had just proclaimed its undying love to me.

No words needed ...

He cradled me in his arms, refusing to let go.

I felt more than grateful because I was in much, much worse shape than he was. Totally spent and unable to do anything beyond bask in the dream of being held tightly against Levan Ivankov's hard form while hot water cascaded down our bodies.

It didn't even register that I spoke, until I heard the words coming out of my mouth, my voice shaky and thick with emotion, "How the hell am I supposed to ever recover from you?"

All I heard was his soft laughter, and the thought of losing him scared me.

https://www.youtube.com/watch?v=WQnAxOQxQIU

I didn't fall asleep.

After we'd taken a quick shower together, with me doing most of the washing as Bianca was too spent to even move, I carried her to bed and tucked her naked body underneath the covers with mine.

She soon drifted off to a deep sleep, while I was left listening to the gentle, even sound of her breathing. I basked in the aftermath of what had been the best sex of my life. In short, I had fucked us both nearly out of our minds, but all I could feel was love. It felt as though my heart had burst open, and fiery, molten lust had trickled down and set the whole of my stomach on fire.

She was even more than I had ever dreamed of. It wrenched

at my heart to think I would have to leave her soon. And our separation could be years. Perhaps even forever.

The light from the moon cast a soft ethereal glow on her. I studied her features, determined to commit all of it to memory. From her beautiful, still slightly damp hair to the sweep of her long lashes as they lay on her cheek. I memorized the slight curve to the tip of her nose, as if it were the most important thing I had to remember in my life.

When she slept, her bottom lip protruded slightly more than the upper one, which gave the impression that she was in the middle of a pout.

My lips stretched into a smile at the thought, and I couldn't stop myself from leaning forward to place a light kiss on her forehead.

Even in her sleep, she moaned and moved towards me.

I felt a bond with her that I never had with another, and I'd felt it from the very first moment I ever laid eyes on her. Then I had let it go, because I didn't trust it.

But I trusted it now. The decision was made the moment I took her from Bogdan's grasp and I was ready to give it all up for her. The feeling I had was very pure. I guess the closest thing to it would be a mother's love. All I knew was that I needed to make sure she was safe, and happy, even if those things happened without me.

She stirred in her sleep, but then blindly turned towards me. She tapped her small hand on my chest and arm as if making sure I was still there then sighed in her sleep.

I felt my gut do a little flip in response.

Oh, Bianca, Bianca, Bianca. How can I keep you?

I buried my face in her neck and breathed in her scent.

I remained there for the longest time, my head full of thoughts on how to clean up the rubble that was slowly piling up at my feet. Before I knew it, the sun had started its journey back into my world.

She awoke when I moved, as though she could sense my restlessness. Her eyelids fluttered open and met mine ...her eyes looked soft and dreamy.

This made me long for many more mornings of her waking up beside me. I almost choked on the emotion.

"Hey," she breathed.

"Hey," I choked.

"What's the matter?" she asked with a frown.

"Nothing," I whispered.

"Are you sure?" She wriggled her body closer to mine and reached up a hand to gently run it down my cheek.

I thought she intended to say something, but I could feel her curves and warmth setting me ablaze ... this was the last thing I needed. Maxim was wrong when he said I was thinking with my dick. When it came to Bianca, it was my heart doing all the thinking. "We're going to Spain today," I informed her, shifting slightly away.

She frowned. "But you were let out on bail. Are you allowed to leave the country?"

"My dad called for me," I explained. "Over the years, we've

cultivated the art of disappearing when needed. I'll get to Spain and return without the wrong people knowing about it."

"Oh," she replied.

I tucked her hair behind her ear. "And since it's a very beautiful and serene place I'm expecting it to give you some space from all the madness here."

"Okay," she said.

Another stretch of silence passed before I spoke again, "I might also not be able to hold onto you, but I'm going to do everything in my power to make sure you're safe."

She instantly went still in my arms. Then she moved, and I was forced to loosen my hold as she rose and sat on her elbows. I knew she was about to demand an explanation, when my phone began to ring.

I turned to the nightstand to glance at it, and couldn't ignore it when I saw it was Maxim.

"I'm in the breakfast room," he said and ended the call.

I kissed Bianca, my teeth lightly pulling on her bottom lip, before I rose from the bed. I knew her eyes were on my naked body as I rounded the bed, and I relished it. I didn't turn around to look at her, because that would only tempt me into getting back into bed with her.

In a few minutes, I was dressed and walking into the breakfast room to meet Maxim.

He was eating a bowl of fruit salad.

I took a seat by his side.

He turned to gaze at me. "Your flight's in two hours," he said. "A few feds are monitoring the house right now, so I've arranged for you to leave in the gardener's service van at 11:35."

"I'm taking Bianca and Aldie with me," I said.

He shook his head, almost in disgust, then stood up and walked away, but when he got to the door, he stopped. "You do know Dad doesn't give a fuck about anyone apart from himself and the business, don't you?"

"That's why I need her with me," I replied. "I need to have my eyes on her at all times."

"And you think putting her in a place where he'll have his eyes on her too is the best move? Why not leave her here? I'll make sure she's safe."

"You're flying to Switzerland tonight, aren't you? So you will not have your eyes on her and you will not be completely sure she will be safe at all times."

"God, I never thought I'd see the day when you became a lovesick fool." Then he walked out of the door.

I stared at his half-eaten fruit bowl. Maxim and I used to be close and now, we were like strangers. It made me sad, but I knew he would come around one day. One day, he would see the shining beauty of Bianca's soul and he would know then why I could never throw her to the wolves.

36

BIANCA

"Holy cow, these things look like mini pussies," Aldie said with a little giggle, as she took a scarlet red, squid burger canapé from the platter held out by the flight attendant.

"You're crazy, you know," I said with a smothered laugh.

"Seriously, look at them," she insisted, showing it to me.

"I suppose it's an improvement on what you usually think they look like," I said dryly.

"Ah yes, pussies look like axe wounds made by the men of Gulliver's island," she said as she popped the burger into her mouth and chewed appreciatively.

I reached out to grab a lobster and avocado canapé. "Thanks," I murmured to the flight attendant.

"You're welcome," she said, with a smile and moved away.

"So anyway, how long are we going to stay in Spain?" Aldie asked.

I turned to gaze out of the plane's window. We were at that altitude where the clouds seemed so close, almost as though you could just step off the plane and right onto them. It was breathtaking. "Well, we didn't exactly have much knowledge of this trip two hours ago, so until this uproar cools down, I suppose."

"And when will that be? It's all the media has been reporting on for the last two days." She leaned in to me. "How is he even able to leave the country? Wouldn't it be illegal?"

I frowned darkly. Aldie was right and I'd been worrying about it too. Why was Levan's father making him take this unnecessary risk?

Aldie saw the expression on my face and changed tack. She patted my arm comfortingly. "I'm probably worrying about nothing. I'm sure if the CIA and Mossad can travel to any country to carry out a hit under false identities then an organization such as the Ivankov's must know exactly what they are doing." She drained the champagne flute she had filled with Pepsi. "Things might look a great mess right now, but damn, it's not so bad when one of the consolation prizes is a trip to Europe in a private plane. I cannot even believe where I am right now."

What I couldn't believe was that I didn't know where Levan was. I had last seen him when he had told me about the trip, and since then I had been led by his staff from the house to the plane.

It didn't feel right at all.

37

I was waiting when they landed. I had arrived much earlier in secret on my false passport and been ushered without incident into the country by corrupt officials.

The sun was shining as I strode towards the plane. As she came down the steps, I arrived at the bottom of them. Her lashes fluttered with surprise and I stared into the enthralling blue eyes of the woman I loved.

"Levan," she called, surprised. "Are you okay?"

I nodded and opened my arms to her.

She came into them and kissed me with a soft, intimate, drawn out caress that had my heart racing. It was incredible the effect this woman had on me. With all the other women I'd ever been with, I became less and less interested as time went on, but with her, the opposite happened. The more I knew her, the deeper into her spell I fell.

"I fell asleep in the plane and dreamed about you," she whispered.

I smiled. "What was I doing in it?"

She placed her hand to my cheek.

My skin felt scorched at the contact. I pressed my hand to hers, and held it in place at the sweet delicious burn.

"I don't remember, but I know you got hurt and I was terrified."

I saw the plea in her eyes for me to keep myself safe, not just for my wellbeing, but for hers. I lifted her into my arms.

"What are you doing?" she squealed and tried to get down.

I wouldn't let her wriggle away. Other men could say confidently, they would carry their girl over the threshold as a bride, but I may never get to carry her again. What little time we had together was precious. I carried her from the last step of the plane, into the waiting car. Aldie got into the front passenger seat while I settled Bianca into the back much to her chagrin.

Going around the other side of the car, I joined her in the back and we were on our way.

Thirty minutes later, we passed quaint villages with medieval architecture and arrived in the town of St. Agaró, on the Costa Brava, headed towards the closed access, gated community where I had spent part of my childhood. The memories were not good ones, and once I left, I had never returned.

Yet, here I was, returning, and bringing my most precious

possession. Despite the tragedy that happened here – as in my mother losing her life here – it was still the safest place I knew to put Bianca.

38

The Ivankov's family's villa was distributed over three floors, and set upon the isolated promontory containing a sprinkling of exclusive homes. We were at the far side of the marina, to the south, and when we arrived at the extensive grounds of the villa, I saw that they had the most picturesque view of a coarse sand beach divided by a large spur of rock, my heart felt at peace.

"That's the Sa Conca beach," Levan informed us.

When we got down from the car, Levan showed us to one of the many reception rooms. It truly felt like I had stepped into an exquisite palace from centuries earlier. It held an air of old world glamor.

The paintings on the wall seemed to be museum quality and gigantic. I felt as though I could walk into them. The upholstery and treasures around the room all told their own tale of just what it meant to be staggeringly wealthy. Beyond that lofty room was a wall of glass doors which had been folded away to let in the island's cool breezes.

"Wow!" Aldie gasped, as she headed over to the low stone balustrade that separated the room from the magnificent cypress trees below and the infinity pool that seemed to float over the bay.

I turned to meet Levan's gaze.

A silent uniformed staffer came and took our luggage.

"They'll move them up to your rooms," Levan said.

"God!" Aldie squealed. "Look at all of this, Bianca. Is it even real? Wow. Is it even possible to be this rich, Levan? And to think you made us think you were a simple college student. What great secrets you kept from us. You're the absolute worst." She turned to give me a mischievous smile. "And how the hell did you fall for Bianca instead of me?"

Levan's phone began to ring then, and he took the call and turned slightly away from us.

I watched as he listened quietly, his gaze expressionless and set far into the horizon. I sensed the cold, hard energy that came over him towards whomever he was speaking to. When the call ended, he quickly excused himself and said he had something important to attend to and we were to amuse ourselves for a while.

I spent a few more minutes with Aldie. Even though she gushed and was wildly appreciative of the beauty and luxury around us, I was unable to even mildly appreciate the paradise I found myself in. Eventually, I decided not to be a killjoy to her obvious delight. What I most needed in the moment was to rest for a while in peace. Maybe think. About Levan, about my father, about Bogdan. About what I would do if Levan ended up in prison because of me.

"I'm going for a nap," I said to Aldie, and turned around to take my leave.

There was no one around to show me the way, but Levan had waved his hand in the direction of the left-hand portion of the second floor and he had also told us to explore the whole house, so I decided to just find my way to the rooms where our bags had been taken to.

I went up the grand marble stairs and felt a little bit like a princess in a fairytale. At the top, I saw what seemed to be the entrance to a massive conservatory full of gorgeous tropical plants. I couldn't resist immediately heading for it. I walked into the plant filled space and wanted to linger – perhaps it would be a better place to think than the bedroom I'd been looking for. A small pond sat in a corner filled with lilies and beautiful red and gold koi. Beyond the glass walls was the breathtaking view of the ocean.

I began to stroll around the miniature fruit trees and the brilliantly colored flowering potted plants. As I stood there admiring the effort that had gone into this garden I heard the voices. They sounded muffled, but I was certain one of the voices was Levan. I was not in the habit of snooping so I quickly walked towards it, with the intention of announcing my presence. I made it to the end of the wonderful garden and spotted a white, glass paneled door. It was shut, but through it, I could see Levan. I didn't however, see who he was speaking to.

For a moment, I wanted to go forward, but then I saw the angry, forbidding look on Levan's face and I knew I shouldn't intrude. But as the voices got a bit louder, I took a step backwards. Then I turned around and my heart lurched into my throat in shock at the sight of the 6ft 4 inch frame that blocked my path.

"Oh my God!" I gasped, slapping my hand across my mouth.

The icy blue, almost soulless eyes of Maxim stared at me expressionlessly.

Levan had told me he was going to Switzerland.

What was he doing here? And why had he come in so silently?

I felt scared he'd inform Levan that I was eavesdropping on him when I had barely even heard a word. Not that I would have understood. They were speaking in Russian. "Hello," I croaked.

He didn't reply.

"Can you move please? I-I need to leav—"

"No, you should stay," he said softly.

I stopped at his detached, solemn voice. It was the first time I think that he had ever spoken directly to me.

"I'll interpret for you."

"No thanks," I said, certain it was a trick of some kind. Besides, I didn't want to eavesdrop on anyone, let alone Levan.

He didn't move. It became clear then that it wasn't a request.

I didn't want to cower and escape through the other way, and at the challenge in his eyes, I knew he expected just that of me, so I swallowed a very painful lump in my throat, and waited it out.

"My brother is speaking to our father," Maxim suddenly said, his gaze on the glass windows. "My father is laughing at him because he wants to leave the family business and live an ordinary life."

Maxim paused, then continued to interpret what his father was saying. "You think you'll ever be able to be free of us? You will forever be a target. I'll give you two months. Two months of thinking that you're an ordinary person, and keeping your eyes day and night on that little gold digger, and you'll be dead! You won't even see the bullet coming. You won't even know who killed you. You'll be like road kill, and perhaps even rot away like one."

I waited to hear what Levan's response would be, but it didn't come immediately. I watched Maxim as his gaze hardened. Then came the reply, "I'll watch my back as best I can. And I'll do the same for hers."

His father's voice rose so much then that I turned away from Maxim, and towards the door.

Maxim kept interpreting, "And how the hell is that going to be possible in New York? Every eye is on you now, after this fucking mess you've created! You didn't even exist before this, and there was a reason why I fought so hard to make it that way, and now you're a big star! Blown up all over the country."

Maxim nodded at me. "Levan said, 'We'll leave the country

... whatever we have to do, but I will keep her safe." He paused and gave his father's reply. "Has that bitch completely turned your brain to fucking mush? In this day and age, there is no corner on earth where you will be safe. Even if we resolve your problem with the authorities. *If* I can find you that dog can too. No matter where you go, you are a dead man."

"I don't care if I die for her." Maxim's voice when he translated Levan's sentence was cold and without emotion.

My throat choked up with emotion.

His father suddenly roared out so loudly, I jumped.

"You fool! What do you think will happen to her after you're dead?" Maxim said, his voice utterly calm.

"Then I will kill Bogdan myself."

Maxim then gave his father's reply. "Ah, I was coming to that. Why haven't you done it? Were you waiting for me or your brother to do your dirty work for you?"

"No, I can take care of my own problems. I wanted to play fair."

"Play fair? Play fair! What are you? A Good Samaritan? God, give me strength. If I didn't know your mother was purer than the driven snow, I would not believe you are a seed from my own loins. Your idea of taking care of your problems is to drag this whole family into the gutter and end yourself in the slammer. Go and eat some food. I am taking over from here."

Then I heard the sound of footsteps receding.

Maxim kept silent after that.

Levan finally followed out after his father. He looked determined as if the conversation was not over yet as far as he was concerned.

"Please don't tell him I was here," I said to Maxim.

"Of course," he said smoothly and moved aside to make way for me.

I ran out of that beautiful garden floating in the sky. I found my way back to the downstairs and found Aldie seated before the most colorful platter of yoghurt, seeds, flowers, and fruits.

"This came after you left. Isn't it great?" she mumbled through her food.

"Let's go for a walk," I said.

She stopped chewing as she noticed the distress in my eyes. "A walk? What's wrong?"

"Nothing, I just need to be out of here for a little bit."

Reluctantly, she rose to her feet, snatching up a handful of strawberries in her hand before she joined me.

39

LEVAN

I STOPPED in my tracks at Maxim's sudden presence in front of me. I scowled at him. "What are you doing here?"

He shrugged. "Trip got cancelled. I thought I'd stop by to see what new troubles you were stirring up."

I shook my head and started to walk away.

He gripped my hand, *hard*. "Dad is right," he said.

"About what exactly?"

"This time? About a lot. You're giving up everything for her, but is she ready to do the same? Is she ready to give up even a fraction of who she is for the future that you want with her?"

"One day, Maxim, you will know what it is to put the life of another before your own."

"Think hard before you go diving down a sheer cliff. There are nothing but rocks down below."

I smiled at him. "One day, Maxim. One day you too, will know that the rocks look like pillows when you feel the way I do."

He walked away from me.

40

BIANCA

We were stopped a few yards from the house by two guards. They were dressed in T-shirts and casual cargo pants, but their eyes gave them away. They were cold and hard. They clearly were trained killers. The wind blew against one of them and I could clearly see the outline of a gun in a holster.

They wanted to know where we were headed. I told them we wanted to go to the beach and they nodded and informed us that they would escort us. The sandy beach was completely deserted, so it wasn't very difficult to find our little sunny corner to settle into. The guards moved about twenty yards away to keep watch.

The sun was setting and for a while, Aldie and I said little, and just stared out into the beautiful sky, lit with hues of pink and purple.

When Aldie held out her palm filled with ripe, red strawberries to me, I just stared at the beautiful fruit, my thoughts back to the conversation Levan had had with his father. It brought home with stone-cold clarity just how much he would have to give up to be with me. How big his sacrifice would be.

Aldie shook her hand to get my attention.

I lifted my gaze and looked at her face.

She stared at me with a concerned expression. "What's wrong, Bianca?"

"What isn't?" I answered. Part of me hoped that she wouldn't ask for details, but another part of me longed for a discussion that would bring me peace and unravel the knots in my soul.

She put her hands in her lap. "Are you going to tell me what's going on or am I going to have to torture it out of you?"

I opened my mouth to speak, but was distracted by a call.

"Hola!"

We both turned and spotted five of Levan's father's staff heading towards us.

At the sight of the picnic baskets and supplies they had in hand, Aldie clapped her hands with delight and jumped up gratefully to accept them.

Two women came over to us with the baskets.

"Master Levan sent this for you," one of them said with a

smile. "We have brought sandwiches, some Spanish dishes, fruit, and sweet wine."

Aldie sighed. "Seriously, Bianca, how is Levan even real?"

I felt my heart tighten with pain. It was wonderful how Aldie had bounced back from her own terrible ordeal but she had no idea what a mess Levan and I were in.

About ten feet behind us, three men who had come with the women, expertly and quickly began to erect what looked like a cabana. Soon, the structure was up and from the thick white poles, hung white billowing curtains. It looked utterly romantic. They left the one facing the sea open and quickly lined it with a thin mattress and cushions.

The women then laid all the food out inside. Once they were done, they walked back together towards the house, chatting away in Spanish.

After shaking the sand off our bodies, we settled into the gorgeous cabana. Aldie reached for the box of chocolate, but I just picked up what looked like a ham sandwich. Pouring us both a glass of rosé wine, I leaned back against the cushions and stared at the technicolor sky. It was truly beautiful and even in my state, I couldn't help but acknowledge it. I looked out to the vast ocean, and allowed the serene rhythm of waves crashing against the shore to calm me.

Aldie continued to dig through the baskets in search of more treasures. Eventually, she found a glass dish of shrimp and moved to join me. She snuggled up close to me, her body warm and familiar.

For a while, it felt like old times again. Only, we had never been anywhere so magical before.

"Now that we are comfortable, tell me everything," Aldie ordered, popping a shrimp into her mouth.

I sighed. "I don't know whether I'm going to make sense to you, but I feel as if I'm holding on so tightly to Levan, however, the problem is he's hanging off a dark abyss by his fingernails, and if I keep holding onto him, we're both going to drop to our deaths."

She turned to me, mouth full and eyes slightly widened at the dark analogy.

I met her gaze with a sad smile. "The worst part is I'm terrified for Levan, but I don't want to let him go."

She swallowed the food in her mouth abruptly. "Bianca, I understand things aren't at their greatest right now, but you need to have a little faith. You don't know because you are not part of the Russian community, but the Ivankovs are actually a force to be reckoned with. I knew that when they rescued me. Bogdan has no idea what he has done pulling the tiger's tail like he has. No matter what it looks like now, Levan will be fine and so will you. This whole mess *will* be resolved, and both of you *will* be okay."

"Even if his issue with Bogdan can be resolved, what about all the others who are not as easy to deal with?" I asked her. "The FBI and the government is a whole other ball game to resolve. He might end up in prison for a very, very long time or he might have to become a fugitive of the law and have to live in hiding forever. Or if that doesn't happen, his association with the *Bratva* will constantly put us at risk like this. And if he were to leave, then he would have to give up his family. I don't want him to do that, but at the same time, I can't give him up." I sighed and looked away.

Aldie patted my hand consoling.

I continued, "Last night he told me that he would hold onto me, which means he has probably made the decision to somehow step away from his family, so that he can be with me in peace. I should be happy but I can't help feeling as though a day would come when he would resent me for that decision."

"Look, if I were you, I'd give it some time," Aldie advised. "Just battle one demon at a time, eh? We might not be able to get all the answers right now, so let's wait until the family rids the world of that mad man, and mark my words they will, then we can move on to the rest."

Her advice sounded so solid. My mom had always said, *cross the bridges as you come to them.* I took a sip of rosé and took a deep breath. "Ok, I'll take it one day at a time."

"Good girl. Now look at that sky. If I had seen this photo on Instagram, I would have thought the photographer had photo-shopped it to death."

I finished the glass.

"Do you want to go back to the house?" Aldie asked.

"No, not yet." I hadn't eaten and the alcohol had gone to my head. I felt relaxed and floaty.

As the sun disappeared and darkness fell around us, staff

came down to the beach to light the lamps around our cabana. They brought blankets with them.

Aldie and I snuggled up together. It was strange and beautiful. I had never experienced such a thing in my life.

I fell asleep to the peaceful ambience of the ocean. I was awakened by a noise and distant laughter in the air. Aldie was holding a lantern and walking away. I wanted to call out to her.

"It's okay. She'll be fine the guards will look out for her," Levan said from next to me.

As usual, a deep emotion trickled into my chest at the mere sight of him. In the golden light of the lamps, he looked dark and mysterious, like the hero of a Victorian novel. The way I had always imagined Heathcliff would look.

My heart lurched, and I instantly rose to my elbows. "Were you watching me sleep?"

"No such luck. I just got here."

I avoided his eyes, as the reminder of my eavesdropping that afternoon returned to haunt me. I wondered if Maxim had told him about it. Before I could stop myself, I leaned forward. Tilting my head, I captured his lips in mine and gave him a soft, lingering kiss.

When I pulled away, I found his eyes gleaming at me.

"Don't start what you don't intend to finish."

I was suddenly open to the challenge. When apart, I thought of everything that was wrong with us, but when he was with me, it became hard to breathe and none of those problems were enough to tear us away from each other. "Well, I am willing to finish anything you want me to," I whispered breathlessly.

He rose to his knees, and his white linen shirt billowed in the salt tinged breeze. He jumped off the bed and in one smooth movement, had picked me up and thrown me squealing in protest over his shoulder. We were on our way back to the house.

"No!" I cried. "I want you to take me on the beach."

"Not tonight, sweetheart," he replied. "The cabana isn't set up for privacy and this is my father's abode after all. I'll get them to set up a more solid structure tomorrow for you."

Even when we got to the house, he refused to put me down, but luckily no guards were in sight to embarrass me. Up those amazing stairs he carried me, not in his arms like a princess, but like a sack of potatoes on his shoulder. In his room, he deposited me on a huge bed. There was an open balcony with a view of the ocean. He shrugged his shirt off his shoulders.

I had decided on the beach to take it one day at a time, and I put that decision to good use. From now on, I wouldn't spoil a minute of what we had with worrying uselessly about the future. I'd gone to the beach in the T-shirt I had flown in with from New York, so I mirrored his action and pulled it over my head. My bra soon followed and I was on my knees on the bed, my full swollen breasts in my hands as I gazed sultrily at him.

"I love you, Bianca," he suddenly said to me.

For a moment, the wind was knocked out of me.

Then the tears came.

Rising to my feet, I dove for this man who meant so much to me and buried my face in his neck. "I love you too, Levan," I choked, breathless at the torrent of emotion that coursed through me. I was filled with gratitude, awe, love, disbelief at my good fortune, and a dizzying excitement at that treasure of a man I could now call mine.

He held on tightly to me when he let himself fall to the bed. Smoothly, he rolled me on to my back and took my breast in his mouth. I didn't even realize he had undressed. All of a sudden, his cock was sliding into me.

I now realized that first entrance, when the walls of my sex expanded to receive his girth, would always floor me.

"Hmmm," he groaned at my tightness. Then he found his rhythm inside me.

I met him, thrust for thrust, breath for breath, heart for heart. It was slow and delicious as I shuddered from pure bliss.

"I fucking love you, Bianca Russet," he breathed. Then he came, accompanied with an almost agonizing groan as he spilled his seed deep inside of me.

I cried and bit down on his shoulder to muffle it all. "I love you. I love you. I love you," I cried again and again.

Our intimacy had stripped me bare of all I was and made me completely willing to submit whole heartedly to this man. To have our hearts as one, in such a way that I didn't know where he stopped and I began. And somewhere deep in me, I wanted his seed to grow inside me. I think I'd always wanted that. It was why I'd never asked for a condom with him. He was the man I'd been waiting all my life for.

Levan was the one.

I never could quite believe the gift that had been given to me. Levan was special and a child from him would be the second best thing that could happen to me. The first was him, of course.

In this moment, I swore I would never let anything threaten the love between us.

41

BIANCA

The next morning, I woke up tangled in sheets that smelled of our union ... uh ... throughout the night.

My cheeks burned at the heated reminder of the numerous ways he had taken me, claimed me, and branded me. My heart felt like it would burst when I thought of the way he had washed my sex soaked and dripping with his cum with a warm towel before he tucked me into bed.

I sat up and looked around the beautiful white room, and felt the despair of the previous day begin to reappear. I immediately buried my face in my hands to tame my overly dramatic mind. I reminded myself of my promise yesterday.

One day at a time, Bianca. One day at a time.

As I sat there repeating those words like a mantra, I heard light footsteps and pushed my hair out of my face to see who it was. My heart skipped when I saw him.

With dampened hair, a naked torso, and a pair of khaki pants that made him look masculine and macho. He'd left the first button open, the slight dusting of hair that covered his groin exposed.

This sight of him was beyond exciting. He looked so good I wanted desperately to fuck him all over again.

He was holding a tray of breakfast.

As he came closer to me, I hooked my fingers into his pants.

"Hey," he protested, placing the tray down.

As I watched, he quickly began to swell beneath those khakis.

I placed my lips on his navel and relished it when he jumped at the touch. I looked up to see his eyes darkening at the tease. Breathing became a hassle. When he tried to pull away, I tightened my hold on the fabric and continued my caress. Following the light trickle of hair down to his crotch, I began to work the buttons down.

His hand covered mine. "We're going to eat first. I chased out all the staff from the kitchen and just spent too damn long whipping all of these for you because I wanted to see you eat something I'd made.

Smiling at the romantic gesture, I splayed my hands over his ass to bring him even closer to me. "Don't worry, this is just my appetizer," I purred.

His grin, that flash of his perfect pearly whites made my blood simmer. I pushed his pants down just enough, and in seconds, the head of his cock was in my mouth. "Hmm." I groaned at his earthy sweet taste and smiled when I felt him begin to flex his hips in response.

He buried his fingers in my hair and I took him as deep as he would go down into my mouth. Then I pulled away, my tongue held drops of his cum. I extended it and showed it to him.

"Arrghh, *fuck,*" he said, starting to lose control. I could feel him quivering in my grip, but before I could suck him into my mouth again, he stepped away from me.

"No," he said in a strangled voice. "Food first! I can't have you collapsing on me again."

I slapped him on the stomach. "I didn't pass out," I complained. "I just fall asleep really quickly. Anyway, I was tired from all the stress!"

"*Yes, really quickly,*" he echoed teasingly, as he put the tray on the bed.

He was still chuckling when I turned my attention to the ambitious breakfast of eggs, sausages, bacon, and perfectly golden toast. By the side, he had cut up an assortment of strawberries, apples, and kiwis, and poured orange juice into a tall glass.

"This looks amazing. Thank you," I commented.

He lowered himself beside me. "No thanks are necessary. I actually enjoyed making it."

I loved his proximity to me. "What about you? Aren't you going to have some too?"

"Nope. I'm just gonna watch my baby eat."

I forked a strawberry and placed it in his mouth. His eyes were fixed on mine, and with a gaze so intense, I froze. Suddenly, the world stopped turning, stopped existing, and it was only us again. He placed his hand on my neck and gently brought my mouth to his. He kissed me and it was filled with the scent and taste of strawberries. It was the sweetest, most intimate kiss I'd ever experienced.

My bones were beginning to melt. To retain some sanity, I pulled away. *How could I ever have thought even for a moment that I could let him go?*

My fingers filtered through his hair. "I'll make you something for lunch."

He shook his head. "We're going out. You, me and Aldie. A friend of mine has a winery about an hour away, so we'll be heading over there for a couple of hours. After that, I'll show you both around the town and we'll grab an early dinner.

"I'm torn," I responded as I nibbled lightly on his lower lip. "Do I just spend the day fucking you, or do I do all those wonderful things you just mentioned?"

He laughed aloud, and captured my lips in another heart stopping kiss. "I'm gonna fuck you until you can't stand tonight, but today I want to show you off. I want everyone to know you're mine. I don't know how long I will be able to do that, so I'm taking that chance today. Anyway, it will give me an opportunity to start making reparations to Aldie for the trauma I put her through."

I wrinkled my nose. "In all honesty, and it did shock me but I don't even think she was even affected that much by it. By nature, she is pretty strong and unflappable. She's been eating everything she can get her hands on since she's been here."

He laughed at this news and picked up a chopped kiwi. "Did I ever tell you that my dream was to produce the best alcohol in the world?"

I nodded at the reminder. "You did, two years ago."

"I think I was inspired from Sebastian, the friend we're going to visit today. His family has produced wine for more than a century and they have a beautiful vineyard. We grew up together here, so every chance I could find I was running around his place and helping out in the summer. I felt free tending the land, more than I ever could at home, or working in the city. I want that again … someday. A vineyard or even a brewery."

"I'll make sure you have that," I vowed.

He raised his head at my comment, the promise in it, not missed at all. That I'd be there. That I'd stay. No matter what.

I leaned forward and sealed it with a kiss.

42

BIANCA

The breakfast was delicious, but I could not forget my appetizer and halfway through I went back to it. An hour later, feeling sated and languorous, I was seated on the counter in his bathroom with Levan positioned between my legs.

His jaw was covered with shaving cream and I was working diligently on his stubble.

He wasn't helping, because he kept staining the tip of my nose with the cream which then I had to keep wiping off.

"Levan!" I scolded.

He only chuckled, which quickly faded when I took the blade and pretended to aim for his hair. He immediately backed away then, his hands in the air in surrender. "Okay, okay," he laughed. "I'll behave."

I was about to continue when his phone began to ring in the bedroom.

Suddenly, everything changed between us. A tension came into his body and he looked behind to glance at it. "I'll be right back, babe," he said, heading towards his room.

A few minutes later, he returned and I knew ... something was very wrong. The way he looked at me had changed. His gaze and stance had shifted from completely and blissfully in love, to strained and almost tormented. Somewhere a dam had broken.

"I have to leave for a quick meeting," he said kissing my forehead in an almost fatherly fashion. Taking the shaver from my hand, he quickly and expertly swiped it along his jaw.

I felt bereft. Again, the outside world had reached into our little magical bubble and was taking him away. I bit my lip as he got to the last piece of unshaved skin. "We're not going to shower together?" I asked, my voice sounded a tad desperate.

He wiped his face with a face towel. "If I get in that stall with you I'm definitely going to miss my meeting," he said, with a grin, but we both knew. There was nothing remotely funny about our situation.

I had been looking forward to spending the day just the three of us in town and meeting Sebastian, but that had gone up in smoke after the phone call. I pulled him closer and slipped my tongue into his mouth, kissing him deeply as though it was goodbye. My legs locked around his hips and I found myself unable to let go till he drew away from me.

I hid my face from him for a moment to get myself together

and came back up with a forced smile. If he could pretend, so could I. "When will you be back?'

He paused. "In a day or two. I'll call you and update you."

"That long? Is the meeting here in Spain?"

He blinked.

I knew instantly. "You have to fly back to New York, don't you?"

"Yes," he said softly.

Always, it was the same. I had to wring even the smallest bit of information from him. Aldie knew more than me. I broke free and jumped down to my feet. "I'll let you get ready quickly then," I said and exited the bathroom, before I broke into tears.

When I arrived in his room, I looked around, close to suffocating and absolutely clueless what to do next. I pulled on my jeans and ran out of the room. I returned to my own room and picked up my phone, but when I tried to connect to the internet, I found out that there was absolutely no available network anywhere. Not even on the balcony.

With a frown at the device, I went over to Aldie's room. She wasn't in so I made my way down to the ground floor straight to the kitchen.

She was sat at the island, making her way through a bowl of mixed nuts. "Hey baby," she called.

"Buenos Días, Señõrita," the two cooks in the kitchen called out as well.

"Buenos Días," I replied with a smile to them, then turned to Aldie. "Hey, do you have internet on your phone?"

She shook her head. "I don't. I asked one of the staff about it last night and he said that it was temporarily down. He said he'd have it fixed and running soon."

I took a seat beside her and wrung my hands together.

"What's wrong?" she asked.

"I think there's trouble in New York and Levan has to go back right now."

She went still. "What trouble?"

"Well, Levan's ensured we won't know what it is by deactivating the internet."

"Whoa," she said. "Take it easy. Where did this paranoia come from? Have you asked him about it?"

"Is there any need to? He's just going to say he's done it to protect me."

"Well he *is* trying to protect you."

"How does fucking keeping me in the dark protect me, Aldie? I want to know. I want him to see me as an equal. Someone who can bear the burden with him. I'm not a little snowflake that will melt at the first sign of heat."

"Protecting you, for Levan, includes not making you worry unnecessarily. He wants it all to be blue skies and rainbows for you, almost as though he blames himself for any hardship you might go through. I say, let him. I'd love it if a man cared that much for me."

"No!" I declared and rose to my feet. "I don't want to add to his troubles. I don't want him to worry whether I am going to be worried. I want to be his rock to know that he can tell me anything and I won't judge, so he will see that I will stand by him. I'm going to go and ask him!"

"Bianca," she called after me.

I was already sprinting from the room. I went back up the stairs to his room and walked in.

Already dressed in a pair of dark trousers and a crisp white shirt, his thick silky hair was still damp from his shower, which always made my toes curl a little. He was removing some documents from the safe in his closet. "Hey," he called and continued with transferring a folder into the briefcase that lay open on the bed. He snapped it and turned to face me. "You alright?"

"There's no internet in the house," I said to him.

"Yes, I know. Island services. I'll get it fixed."

"When?"

His phone began to ring then. "Just a second," he said, taking the call. He listened to what the person on the other line was saying, then spoke, "I'll call you back in a few minutes." Ending the call, he came over to place a kiss on my cheek.

I placed my hand to his chest and held him away. "I'm not trying to start a fight with you, especially since you're leaving right now, but it's not okay that you're deliberately restricting access to the internet so that Aldie and I won't be able to figure out what's going on in New York."

I thought he'd deny it, but he didn't.

"I'm not a child, Levan. This concerns me! This is my life too. You are my life. Whatever happens to you, happens to me."

"I know that," he said. "But right now only a handful of us know that you're involved and I'd like to keep it that way. The more contact you have with the outside, the more likely it will be that you or Aldie will accidentally slip-up and bring attention here. I'll handle the things that I can and then when its time, I'll tell you about the things that I cannot."

"I want to help, Levan."

"And I'll let you, when it's *needed*. Not yet. Please trust in me. I'll be back soon and then I'll tell you everything that's going on. I promise."

With my heart feeling like it was splitting in two, I let him kiss me again, and walk out of the room.

43

LEVAN

I walked off the tarmac and tossed my briefcase into the town car. As I slid in, I found my brother awaiting me in the backseat.

A folder sat in his lap and he closed it. "Welcome back," he murmured.

"Yeah. It's great to be back," I said bitterly.

"Is the love wearing off already?" he taunted.

I turned to him angrily. "I don't need this shit. What the fuck am I doing here? Why did I even have to leave the country and jump bail if I was just going to come back in time for my hearing anyway?"

"It was easier with you out of the way."

I felt my temper rise with the high-handed way my brother

was dealing with the situation at hand. "So, what's going to happen now?"

"You'll have to suffer the indignity of being handcuffed again, but it'll just be a temporary inconvenience."

"What do you mean temporary? Are you going to be able to get me out?"

"Of course," he said confidently, looking directly at me. "I'm not going to watch you rot away, especially for something you didn't do." For a moment, the shield was gone and in its place was the brother I knew once loved me, beyond anything else in this world.

"But what can you do at this stage? Sarah Dale has implicated me so publicly that nobody, no matter how corrupt will touch this case and try to help."

He smiled. "Have faith little brother. I didn't come this far and run this operation all these years without keeping a trick or two up my sleeve."

I looked at him curiously. "What trick are you talking about?"

"I spoke to Sarah before her press conference," he explained calmly. "And we agreed that she would feed the press to an easily disproven pack of lies. They would buy it and so would Bogdan, but every bit of evidence in her testimony can be dismantled and reversed as soon as her grandson is found."

I stared at my brother in wonder. Even when I was very young, I was impressed by him. He seemed almost godlike to me then and now, I fully understood how he had taken my father's blood drenched criminal organization and over time, turned it into one of the most successful legal enterprises in America.

"Bogdan seems to have dropped off the surface of the earth, but have no fear. Time is our friend and the bastard's worst enemy," Maxim said. "Every minute that passes brings his death closer.

I exhaled with relief. "So where are we going now?"

"Back home so that your bail conditions remain unbreached and I have organized a distraction to get you inside unnoticed. Thereafter, you'll leave with the patrol car that will be sent to take you to the courthouse. You'll meet McKinsey who'll be awaiting you there," he said referring to my lawyer. "She's trying to put everything together for the moment Sarah makes her announcement."

I looked out of the window onto the buzzing intersection of Union square that we were riding through. I didn't love New York. I knew then that I wanted no part of this city. I wanted to take Bianca and move to a small town where we could raise our family without this madness. I turned towards Maxim. "I'm sorry. I really am sorry for all the trouble I caused you. I never wanted that."

His lips twisted. "I know."

"No matter what happens, I'm not going to be part of the organization anymore."

"I know." And this time his smile was real.

I realized he was relieved because he too, knew I was not cut out for this brutal world my father and he occupied.

Three hours later, I arrived in the back of a patrol car to the courthouse to meet a flashing storm of reporters and stoic law enforcement officials. Two police officers were flanked by my sides and my hands were handcuffed. A quick look back from the commotion and I saw my brother leaning against the SUV parked across the street. His eyes were on me and when our gazes met, he winked at me.

I winked back.

Then I straightened my back, ignoring all the microphones and recorders shoved in my face. I walked up the endless flight of stairs to the criminal court.

I didn't expect any leniency to be given to me as I settled into my role as a defendant and listened as my attorney and other officials of the state stepped forward for my arraignment.

The room was full, and there were no familiar faces present except Yuri as the team had been ordered to stay low.

My indictment was quite robust, with accusations of my family's conglomerate managing to penetrate layers of the state's apparatus. It was considered a severe threat, especially given my family's Russian background.

The charges were presented as a "dizzying array of criminal schemes, attempting to commit fraud, shipment thefts from cargo ships, federal robbery charges, casino fraud, money laundering, international banking fraud, extortion, wire fraud, credit card fraud, and identity theft."

Well Maxim, that card up your sleeve had better be good.

44

BIANCA

"**C**an you believe this?" I asked in disbelief. "Can you see all the things they're charging him with?"

Aldie turned away from the large TV screen in Levan's room we had been camped in front of for the whole day. Once I'd learned that Levan had switched the Internet service back on, we had both ignored everything around us. We spent all our time scouring the internet for every scrap of news on his arraignment and updates on his now case.

I couldn't believe he had left for something as serious as this, and hadn't told me but I guess giving me access to the Internet meant, he knew I would find out anyway. Why the hell didn't he just tell me? I could have dealt with it. "He said he would be back in a day or two," I said to her. "He keeps lying to me." I sunk deeper into the covers and tried to breathe in Levan's scent.

She rubbed my shoulder in sympathy. "I told you before you should trust Levan and if not Levan, then definitely his father and brother. They are not going to let Levan end up in prison."

I picked up my phone again for the umpteenth time in the last hour, and looked at it silent, completely void of any contact from the man I most needed to speak to. I thought of calling Maxim, but I had no clue of how to reach him, short of hounding the guards in the villa for his number, and I doubted they would give it to me anyway. Moreover, would he even be willing to speak to me? I knew he held me responsible for the storm that was brewing, threatening to destroy his world.

Then I called my father. Maybe he would know something about where Bogdan could be hiding. Maybe I could help Levan that way. But it was no use because my father was still in hiding and did not answer his phone. Then I suddenly realized that because I had caused so many problems when I overreacted the last time when Aldie was taken, the best I could do for everyone now was to be calm.

I somehow managed to fall asleep and when I awoke, it was past midnight.

Aldie was still fast asleep beside me. I hadn't cared to eat anything all day and it felt as if my stomach was about to cave into my skeleton from sheer hunger. Without waking her up I rose, and began to make my way to the ground floor kitchen.

Scary was an understatement for traipsing about in such a massive house, unaccompanied, and at such an hour of the night. But I braved it and switched on the light of the kitchen. I seated myself at the island with my laptop, a bowl of cereal, and my gaze on the update of Levan's case from CNN's international website.

My phone suddenly began to ring and when I saw it was from an unidentified number, I immediately picked it up, thinking it would be Levan. "Hello? Levan," I said eagerly into the receiver and held my breath for the response.

When no reply came through, a cold chill began to crawl up my skin. I dared not even breathe as I held the phone tightly against my ear.

For a few more fearful moments, there was no response, then I heard the voice that I could recognize in a heartbeat, distant, but unmistakable. It was my father. "Bianca," he called pitifully.

I swung into action. "Where are you right now? Do you know where Bogdan might be?"

There was another pause.

"Dad," I called. "Dad?"

I heard the laughter in the background then and the spoon clattered from my fingers to the floor. I shut my eyes as my heart sank.

This was trouble, very big trouble and the days from here on, would only get darker.

"I don't think I need to introduce myself to you, do I my angel?" Bogdan said into the speaker.

It felt like worms were crawling under my flesh. "What are you doing with my father?"

"You don't get to ask the questions," he said. "I hear you're in Spain, whisked away by that bloody fool. You chose the wrong man, my angel."

"Bogdan, what the *fuck* do you want with my father?" I growled into the phone, now on my feet, and pacing restlessly up and down the cold granite floor.

"I want nothing with him," he responded. "All I want is with you, so listen very carefully. You have twenty-four hours. Get back here in time, or the next message I send to you will be where you can retrieve your father's corpse from."

"Don't come!" I heard my dad yell out in the background. "Don't you come here, Bianca. Do you hear me—"

He cut the call then, and with a scream of frustration and horror, I flung the phone away from me. It smashed into a wall and shattered to the ground. I stared at the destroyed pieces, my chest heaving dangerously.

My mind was so full of fury, I saw nothing while my soul was brimming with the need to kill that monster. To end him for the absolute and complete nightmare he had turned my life into. Yes, I would go to him. And I would somehow find a way to kill him, whether I poison him, stab him, it didn't matter. Then my dad, Levan and I could be free to live our lives.

I turned around to exit the kitchen ... *and froze.*

Someone stood in the doorway.

For a moment, I thought that it was one of the guards, but as he moved out of the shadows and into the light I saw that it was the Don himself. It was as if I was looking at Levan in about fifty years. Only there was no kindness in his eyes. He had kept out of sight and I had wondered just when I might meet him and this was probably the worst possible moment as I was still shaking with fury.

"Come with me," he said.

At first, I didn't know whether to follow him, but then I realized that meeting with him was not something I could put off. If Levan were to be in my life then he would be too. I remembered his less than favorable opinions of me only a few days earlier. And if he'd wanted to get rid of me, he could easily have done so by now.

Under normal circumstances, I would have been more nervous standing before Levan's father as he sat behind the heavy oak desk in his gigantic study, but right now not only my own father's life was at stake but also Levan's.

He studied me quietly, and it made me wonder if it was an intimidation tactic, but I was too distraught for it to work. I stepped forward and cut to the chase, "Can you please get me back to New York? I have an emergency to attend to."

"Is it an emergency bigger than the mess you've put my family in?" he asked calmly.

The accusation cut deep. I took a deep breath, and put my hands together in a sincere plea. "I am so sorry that my love for your son has caused all this to happen. I never even dreamt things would deteriorate to this extent, but I'm going to try my best to fix it all for everybody."

"Really?" he asked, a note of mocking awe in his voice, "How are you going to do that?"

"First of all, I need to get to my father. The man that ... the man causing all of this trouble and tormenting Levan has him."

He kept silent and gave the impression of listening intently.

So I went on, "If we can get to him, then we will be able to find the Solicitor General's grandson, and that will help Levan's case too."

His question was simple, "So are you actually trying to save your father, or to free my son?"

I stopped. It was as though my brain had scrambled to a halt and when a response didn't come forth, I blinked. "What do you mean?"

"English is your first language, is it not?"

At his rudeness, I straightened my back. The truth was my only real interest was in saving Levan somehow. My father had made his bed and it was time he lay on it, but I was not going to be disloyal to my father in front of this stranger. "I'm going to help them both."

He watched me, quietly, and then rose to his feet. My

instinct was to back away, but I caught myself before he could see it.

He headed to the shelf of nameless books that looked more like props or encyclopedias. With one hand, he cleared the books away, and I jumped as they fell to the ground with a loud thud. With the books gone, I could see a safe which he opened. I wondered what was in there.

He pulled out a jewelry box and came around to the front of his desk. He opened the box, placed it on the table beside him and he leaned against the desk.

From where I stood, I could only see that it was either a necklace, or a bracelet. I couldn't tell.

He held my gaze and addressed me. "I met the mother of my boys when I was sixteen. I'd just gotten paid from beating up a boy three years my senior because his parents couldn't pay their debt and I was walking down the road. And there she was. Her mother was selling blini by the side of the street. It was her laughter that stopped me. Ah, she was beautiful then. Next to me was a jewelry shop and I walked in and bought this bracelet for her. Then I walked up to her, gave her this bracelet and told her I was going to marry her."

"Two years later, I married her ... but ten years ago, I *killed* her."

Something so painful struck me in the chest, it took my breath away.

He allowed his words to sink in, and then went on, "Levan has taken your hand, and there are only two ways it can end. Either he kills you or you kill him."

I didn't even know what to say. I just wanted to leave. I couldn't breathe. "I will never hurt Levan—"

"You already have. He's locked up right now, behind bars, and it's all for your sake. I can't stop him from giving his life to you, but I will tell you this. The day you turn your back on him, is the day that I will end you. And you won't see it coming."

He turned to the box by his side. "I want you to give this bracelet to Levan the moment you see him in New York. It means a lot to me and him, so do not for a moment let it out of your sight until you see him. Do not for a moment, let it out of your sight. He will understand what it means when he receives it. A plane will be ready to take you back to America in three hours." With that, he straightened and walked out of the study.

His words were reverberating through every fiber of my being. Then my legs began to work, and I headed over to the table. I picked up the bracelet and looked at the thing that once belonged to Levan's beloved mother. I fastened the emerald and gold band around my wrist, then left the study.

45

I realized that I needed to call Maxim and when I approached one of the guards he said he could not do so, but he would have Maxim call me.

After the mess previously and how annoyed he was the last time I pulled a disappearing act, I wasn't about to make the same mistake again. I waited around anxiously for Maxim's call.

Some thirty minutes later, he called. I had insisted that Aldie remain in Spain so when Maxim's town car pulled up beside the plane at the private airport we had landed at, I was alone.

One of his men held the back door open for me and I slid in. Restlessly, I tapped my fingers against the seat as the car moved smoothly towards Levan's house. The moment the car came to a standstill, I jumped out and headed straight to the kitchen.

Gloria was there. "Hello there," she greeted cheerfully. As usual, she gave no indication that she was surprised by my sudden appearance.

I gave her a polite smile before heading over to the refrigerator to grab a bottle of water.

"Are you hungry? Can I prepare some food for you?" she asked.

"No, thank you. I'm fine." I smiled back at her and downed more than half of the bottle. My nerves were shot to hell, but I didn't have time to dwell on how I was feeling. I only had a few hours left to get to Bogdan and my father.

Quickly, I headed straight towards Levan's office. Two of his guards stood outside. I knew they weren't fond of me, given all the stunts I had pulled in the past and landed them in deep trouble with their boss. They inclined their heads coldly at me. I walked past them and knocked smartly on the door.

"Come," Maxim called.

I pulled the handle down and walked in.

He was seated behind the desk, but even so, the luxury and danger that filled the air around him was impossible to miss. It made me wonder if any woman would ever be able to tame him. He lifted his cold, unreadable gaze up to me and I held my ground as I had already learned that to survive the tigers in this household, one had to do that.

"The bracelet," he said.

I looked down at the jewelry I'd almost forgotten was on me.

"Your father gave it to me," I replied. "He insisted I hand it directly over to Levan the moment I saw him. He said that it belonged to—"

"I know who it belonged to," he cut me off.

I snapped my mouth shut. I still had a hard time believing the cold and psychopathic way his father had told me about their mother's death. I thought my family was dysfunctional, but this was one hell of a peculiar family.

Maxim rose to his feet and came around the table to lean against it just as his father had earlier back in Spain. "I need Bogdan alive. At least until we can find the kid. That's Levan's only way out right now."

"What about my dad?"

"My priority is my brother," he informed me icily. "What's yours?"

My response remained the same. "Both of them. The man I love and the man that fathered me."

"Noble," he nodded mockingly. "Especially given he all but sold you to an insane criminal."

"He is still my father. Trouble or not, I can't have another, so I will have to make do."

He watched me for a few more seconds before speaking again, "You will call Bogdan and you will ask him for a meeting location. He will already suspect by now that we are well aware of your movements since you wouldn't have been able to leave Spain without us anyway, so he will be on high alert. He will arrange for some complicated pick-up, but we will have to work around that. Ready to call him now?"

I nodded as I pulled my new phone out of my pocket and dialed the number that Bogdan had called me with earlier. I didn't know if I would make it out from Bogdan's lair alive, but I prayed he wouldn't harm me. He seemed to want me with a desperate obsession and I truly wondered what he saw in me, or why he would risk so much and sacrifice so many lives just to have me. Maybe it was some kind of pissing contest with Levan. I imagined he would not have been so desperate for me if Levan had not shown he wanted me too. Maybe it was truly a male thing as in the wild when two male lions fight ferociously over the female.

I listened to the ringing tone, loud on the speaker.

"Angel," his voice boomed into the room. "I have been informed you are back from your trip. My regards to you, Maxim."

I looked at Maxim, but he indicated with his hand that I should continue.

"Where are we meeting?" I asked through gritted teeth.

"Well," he answered. "I hope for your sake and that of your father's, that you will be coming alone. Otherwise, the crown prince will have two gravesites to visit when he comes out of prison. If he ever gets out!" His voice boomed with an insane laughter that hurt my ears. Just as suddenly, as his laughter began it ended and his voice cut to the business at hand, "I will text you the address. Be there at 9pm sharp and you will be picked up. If anyone follows you, your father is a dead man." He ended the call.

My phone buzzed and I raised it to read what he had sent aloud, "49 East Mosholu Parkway. The Bronx."

Maxim stretched out his hand.

I placed my phone on it.

"We have two and a half hours," he said.

46

BIANCA

The meeting point turned out to be an abandoned school in the Bronx. I could see this information didn't sit well with Maxim.

"Isn't that too easy for us?" I asked. "I mean, it's quite an active neighborhood. There are homes and stores, and even a police station just a few minutes away.

"Yes, much too easy," he murmured. "I think he might have something else planned, but we won't know until we get there."

"So we're just going to head over there without a plan?" I asked.

"We aren't, you are."

I was suddenly afraid. It seemed as if Maxim didn't have a plan at all. I suddenly realized that giving me to Bogdan was the perfect solution to all his problems. The kid gets found,

Levan gets off more lightly, I get thrown out of the picture, especially if I get killed.

He stood.

I turned to look at the clock on the wall. It was about twenty minutes to 9.00 p.m. I swallowed painfully and rose to my feet too. Well, I didn't need him to fight my battles. I would do it on my own. I was fighting for Levan now. And my father.

When he exited the room, I trudged along behind him.

Ten minutes later, I was alone in a taxi and headed towards the venue. We soon arrived in front of the gates.

I called Bogdan once again, for further instructions.

"The gate is unlocked," he said. "Walk in … alone."

"And then what?" I asked.

"And then you go up to the top floor. It doesn't matter what room you enter."

"And then what?" I asked.

"And then you *wait!*" he growled, and the phone disconnection beeped.

I fought with all my willpower not to look around me since it was quite possible I was being watched by Maxim's men. I walked up to the cast iron gates and saw that the chain around them had been cut. I went through the gate, crossed the yard, and opened the wooden front door. It was thick and heavy, but unlocked. A musty smell came from inside and it seemed dim, but I could still see my way around.

I spotted the staircase by the side and went up it, carefully. As I went higher, it became darker, and I had to use the light on my phone to provide some illumination. I arrived at the top floor and looked around, clueless and extremely wary. Something was very, very wrong. My father wasn't here. Yet, I got the feeling I was being watched. I looked at the ceilings for cameras and saw none.

Suddenly, the air was pierced with the scream of police sirens, and I turned sharply towards the sound, wondering what was going on.

It drew closer and closer as it broiled up a sour feeling within me. I rushed through the nearest door I could find and hurried over to a broken window. From where I stood, I had a bird's eye view of the ambush. In the distance, a fleet of police vehicles had surrounded Maxim's men's two vehicles.

I couldn't breathe as I watched the commotion, the screaming of the police officers I could hear through a broken window. As Maxim's men came out of their vehicles with their hands up in the air—it dawned on me.

Bogdan had separated me, so that he could isolate me. The police would take Maxim's men with them and then I would be all alone and without protection. He knew all along Maxim would have eyes on me and so he must have come up with some story for the cops to grab Maxim's men.

With a gasp, I turned around, ready to run for my life, but I was suddenly smacked so hard across the face that the excruciating pain was like a flash of bright light across my eyes. I was flung into a row of wooden tables and chairs. I began to crawl away frantically and swore as a steely hand closed around my ankle.

Another blow fell on my head and I could feel myself blacking out.

The last thought in my head before darkness took over ...

I would probably never see my Levan again!

47

"What? She's not in Spain!" I stared at Viktor across the glass from me with an uncontrollable fury. I could feel myself swirling out of control.

He lowered his head, sorrowful.

Before I could catch myself, I was out of my seat. My open palm smacked so hard against the glass, he jumped and almost fell out of his chair. It toppled behind him.

"What the fuck do you mean she's gone?"

A couple of burly guards approached me.

"Hey, Ivankov! You're out of line! Another episode like that and you're going back to your cell"

I didn't heed them and they grabbed me, twisting my arms behind my back while locking metal cuffs around my wrists.

"Are we going to have a problem man?" One of the guards asked.

I barely heard him, my focus solely on the apologetic look on Viktor's face. I could see the fear in his eyes. "Who fucking let her leave Spain?" I howled as the guards dragged me away from the visitation room.

Other prisoners and visitors were looking on, curious about what was going on.

"Get me Maxim! Fucking get me Maxim!" I roared.

They dragged me through the corridor and I let them. I felt empty, alone and without control. *Where was she? Why did Maxim let her leave?* My heart felt like a stone in my body. Everything had gone wrong. So fucking wrong.

The guards returned me to my cell, and as the bars slid shut before me, I dropped to my knees and prayed to a God I did not believe in.

48

BIANCA

https://www.youtube.com/watch?v=KL6vbTCOEGU

I was spread out, tied up on a cross made of wood and pipe while hung up on the rough wall of a large empty warehouse. Surrounded by windows, I could see through the dirty glass panes and recognized the Williamsburg Bridge as well as the surrounding cobblestone Dumbo. My father was in the same room, but I couldn't bear to look at him, and neither could he me.

He was seated just a few feet from me, bloodied and battered, with his head hanging low. I could see Bogdan and his handful of thugs who appeared to be talking about something.

I was past humiliation, my clothes were in tatters after being ripped from my body. My lips bruised and bloody from the blows I had thus far received.

"Ah, the Princess is awake." Bogdan came over to me, dragging the legs of an iron chair against the concrete floor and took his seat right before me. "Do you know," he asked, "the difference between an offering and a sacrifice?"

I couldn't hear him properly. It must have been that blow to my head. A ringing sound kept clanging in my ears. As I looked down at him from my Jesus-like position, I thought of Levan again. I was glad I loved him. No matter what happened now to me, he would know. I loved him with all my heart.

"Both involves surrender," Bogdan said. "One is mandative, or is it mandated. This language is not easy for me. Anyway, the other is a gift."

Tears fell from my eyes for the first time that evening. I knew then I was going to be sacrificed to this piece of shit before me. I was right. I was nothing to him. It was a pissing contest after all, and he had won.

He went on, "Now, I want to ask you, why was I never good enough for you? What do I lack that that kid you threw yourself to does not? He cannot even protect you. Now you're nothing but a sacrifice, for my dignity, and my pleasure, but it is even sweeter than my wildest dreams because in one fell swoop, I get to destroy the Ivankov's. For years, they behaved as if they were better than me. They aren't and they're about to find that out." He turned to look at my father. When he saw his head still hanging, he signaled to one of his men, and they moved.

I heard my father's excruciating grunt of pain at the blow across his head. Then he was forced to lift his head up.

My gaze moved to Bogdan, and when he turned to meet the hate in my eyes, he smiled. "Your father is not too bad a man. He gave you to me ... but you didn't want me, and now here we are. You are making me kill a good man because you are a stupid, ungrateful bitch!"

He pushed away from the chair to his feet in anger, and walked towards my father.

My mouth moved before I could stop myself, "Don't hurt him," I pleaded. "I'll do whatever you want, just let him go."

Bogdan immediately stopped and looked at me. His smile was blinding. "She speaks!" he exclaimed. "A clap of hands boys," he called to his minions in the shadows.

They quickly cackled out in laughter and claps.

He came to me then, and placed his hands on my cheeks, his lips barely an inch away from mine, his nauseating breath all over my face. "An ungrateful bitch you surely are, but you're so beautiful."

"Please let him go," I pleaded.

He gripped my face hard, and gazing into my eyes, vengefully asked, "What do I have to do to get this much love from you? He has done nothing for you and yet ... what do I fucking have to do?"

"Nothing. I'll do whatever you want."

"Then kiss me," he said and he crushed his lips painfully on my swollen ones. I let him kiss me. When his sour tongue thrust through my lips I wanted to gag, but I sucked it.

Anything, anything to save my Levan and stop him from killing my father right in front of me. This was the only way I was going to be able to take him unawares.

He noted my acceptance, my willingness even, and could not contain his pleasure. He watched me, and seemed to be looking at me with a different set of eyes. There was pride that in front of his men, I was bending to him. "We might just ... we might just be able to turn this around ... and find our way back. Imagine, you on my arm and the Ivankov's rotting away, unable to do absolutely anything about it. But you fucked the pretty boy," he complained. "And for that, you'll never be more than a dog to me. Still, I like dogs."

I remained silent.

He stared at me. "Are you a dog?"

I slowly died inside as I nodded obediently. One way or another, I was going to kill this man. It would be a favor to the rest of the world. Men like him shouldn't exist. He was a monster.

"Yes, I like dogs," he repeated as he gazed hungrily at my breasts. He came close and bit my nipple through my clothes, so hard I screamed with pain.

He laughed. "Bring her down," he roared, wild excitement filling his eyes.

Two of his men rushed forward to do as they had been ordered.

I fell into his arms, unable to stand on my own.

"Leave!" He roared to them, brazen lust burning in his gaze. He lowered me to the floor and pulled my legs apart.

I didn't turn away as his hands went to the buckle of his pants.

49

The door was pulled open, and I jumped to my feet.

"Come on. You're free," the guard said, moving back from the doorway.

"What?"

"Come on, Ivankov. I haven't got all day."

Quickly, I followed him.

My lawyer was waiting outside. "We'll speak later, but Maxim has arranged everything and he will explain everything to you himself," she said.

Silently and impatiently, I went through the procedure of getting out of jail. Then I headed out to the front metal doors that unlocked I hoped for the final time and walked towards the SUV waiting for me.

Viktor immediately jumped out of the car and hurried over to me.

"Where is she?" I asked as he met me.

The anger inside of me was boiling so violently it was hard for me to even contain it. "Boss told us to tell you to call your father. That he'll know where she is."

I frowned, a new fear hitting my chest at what that could possibly mean? Viktor handed over a phone to me and I was almost afraid to take it. Did this mean my father had a hand in all of this? Had he been the one to send her out of Spain and back here?

I dialed my father's number, and moved aside to speak privately to him. "Where is she?"

There was a moment of silence, and I shut my eyes.

"She's at a warehouse in Brooklyn. I've just sent the location to Mikhail. Go quickly. Maxim is already on his way there."

I jumped into the car, fear coiled up in the pit of my stomach and we were on our way.

https://www.youtube.com/watch?v=TdWEhMOrRpQ

I rushed to my father's side.

His face was turned towards me, and with each moment that passed his breathing grew more and more shallow. He was dying.

My face was soaked with tears and so were his.

"I'm sorry," he whispered. "I'm so sorry."

I brushed my hands softly over his bald, bloodied head, and placed a trembling, wet kiss on it. He had saved me.

Bogdan had been a breath away from raping me, when he used up the last bit of strength he had and somehow, through his own pain he set himself free, picked up the heavy metal chair, and swung it so ferociously at Bogdan's head I heard his skull crack.

The consequences were deadly.

Bogdan's men heard the sound of their boss screaming, and immediately burst in. They instantly fired, hitting my father in the stomach and he had collapsed to the ground next to Bogdan.

Frantically, I tore strips of my clothes and tried to tie up his wound so the bleeding would stop, but the material was getting thoroughly soaked and blood was seeping out from my makeshift bandage.

He was dying.

"Don't die, Dad," I whispered, but he was too gone to hear me.

Bogdan's men appeared confused when we all suddenly heard a deafening commotion beyond the warehouse. The few men left inside with us instantly hurried out, their guns cocked, their steps pounding against the concrete floor. There were shouts outside in Russian, and when a gunshot rang out, I kissed my father's bloodied cheek, and put my ear to listen to the faint sound of his almost undetectable breathing.

Tears poured down my cheeks.

I wanted to move my father away from this terrible place, but I knew that if I did, he wouldn't make it anywhere. I'd seen enough movies to know that a gunshot wound to the stomach was deadly. I looked ahead to the mangled chair he had broken upon Bogdan's head, and thought perhaps I should finish the job now. My head said kill Bogdan and end it all, but my heart was afraid that if I left my father's side, someone might come in and shoot him. So I moved as close as I could to him, and as carefully as I could, put my body over his as a shield.

Another gun went off, the sound reverberating and bouncing off the walls of the massive space. I shut my eyes, and prayed for us both, too afraid to look beyond.

Perhaps Maxim had found a way to send someone after me. I turned around then, too afraid to hope and watched the door. As I stared at it, someone burst through.

I heard his voice before I saw him.

"Bianca!" he called.

For a moment, I was certain I was hallucinating. He couldn't be here!

"Bianca!" he called again.

"Levan? Levan!" I screamed and rushed to my feet. I ran towards him.

He caught me and held me tightly in his arms. All I could do was sob, the choking sounds emanating from my throat sounded like I was dying.

"Baby," he muttered as he held tightly onto me, my head cradled in his hand. "Sweetheart, it's alright. I'm here, you'll be fine."

I pulled away. "My dad," I said and pulled him towards my father. "We need to get him out of here. Right now! He's been shot and he's losing a lot of blood ..." My voice broke. "I'm afraid he might not make it."

"Viktor!" Levan roared as we hurried over to my father.

I crouched next to my father as Levan inspected the injury.

"It's bad but he'll live," he said to me, before he called out to more of his men, "Mikhail! Olav, he needs to be taken to a hospital right now."

I watched as they all lifted my father carefully and carried him out of the warehouse. I went with them, trying my best to keep calm but it was close to impossible. We passed four bodies on the floor. They were bleeding out. I recognized them as Bogdan's men and barely gave them a second thought.

The moment they got him in the car, Levan caught me and pulled me along to another vehicle.

At that moment, two more SUV's drove up. Maxim came out of one of them. He walked over to us. "Is he still in there?" he asked his brother.

"Yes."

"Good. I will take care of it all from here." Then he looked at me and gave a small smile. "You did well. Now can I have the bracelet back?"

"What?"

He shrugged. "You didn't really believe my father would give you a family heirloom, did you? It's just a tracker."

I took it off and gave it to him.

He started walking towards the warehouse.

"Let's go," Levan said and we got into the vehicle and drove off.

51

LEVAN

https://www.youtube.com/watch?v=z5i9vT8wGY8

Three hours later, Bianca's dad was out of surgery, and she was so tired she managed to knock off to sleep on the second bed I'd ordered to be put into her father's room.

Leaving two of my men outside the room, I drove to the marine terminal of Port Newark. Upon arrival, I was greeted by an entourage of four SUV's and five of our men awaiting me.

Viktor immediately ran up to me and pulled open my door. Then he began to lead the way towards the specific container amidst the thousands arrayed on the port.

"What's his state?" I asked.

"He's nearly out. Boss did quite the number on him."

"Where is Maxim?"

"Waiting," he answered.

I arrived at the container to find it surrounded by more silent guards in the shadows. The moonlight up above was more than enough to illuminate the sight of my brother standing nearby with his phone pressed to his ear.

I went into the container.

Bogdan was on the ground ... unmoving and nearly unrecognizable. He looked mangled, his face swollen, and his eyes shut tight. There was a pool of blood under him. I frowned. With a dark look at Maxim, I bent down and pressed two fingers to his neck. I released a breath of relief when I confirmed he was still alive.

I turned to Maxim and waited for him to get off the phone.

He ended the call and came in. "They've got Sarah's grandson. He was hiding him in some trailer park in Connecticut. Luckily, they fed him well and he only has a couple of bruises, so he should be fine after a little while."

"Good," I said.

"Well, little brother. Looks like you're in the clear now. I'll get rid of him and you can forget any of this ever happened."

"Don't lay your hands on him again," I said, with a tremor in my voice. "He's mine from here on out."

Maxim's chuckle was dark. "Why, Levan, that's not like you at all. What happened to forgive and forget?"

"He doesn't deserve a quick death ..." I growled.

"Well, that is true but whilst I know you want to finish him and I am sure you would, I can't let you, I'm afraid. I don't want this piece of shit to stain the new life you are about to embark on."

His words pained me more than he knew and I didn't want to listen. "It's not right, Maxim, I caused all this not you."

"Remember your vineyards? You've done all this to keep your woman so that's what's ahead for you. This is not you, little brother. Go now to Bianca and leave me to finish this."

I stared at him and eventually accepted that he was right. I looked down at that pile of dung at my feet.

With a deafening grunt, thick with all the trouble he had caused me, I kicked his ribcage.

A choking sob sounded from his throat, and he made a coughing, gurgling sound. "Oh, Lord, forgive me my sins," he begged hoarsely.

The prayer sent a fresh surge of fury into my body. He wanted forgiveness? What of all the women he had made suffer? I put my hand out and an iron pole was placed in it. I swung it into him, my roars of fury ringing out into the night air.

Then I was finished. I turned away from the past and to thoughts of Bianca.

～

I returned to the hospital, opened the door, and Bianca lunged to a sitting position to see who it was.

Her father was still unconscious as I walked up to her and sat on the bed next to her. I pulled her into my arms.

She threw her arms around me, and held tightly onto me.

I could feel, without needing to hear her speak, her desire, her desperation to have me with her. "I'm here," I assured her. "I'm here, baby." I got onto the bed and pulled her to my chest so she could rest against me. "I'm sorry I wasn't there," I apologized. "I'm sorry I let him hurt you. I'm so very sorry."

"It wasn't your fault," she said immediately. "I wanted to go. I wanted to help you and Dad. Even if he had raped me, it wouldn't have been your fault."

Everything in me stilled. I hadn't allowed myself to think about what had happened to her. I brushed my hand up and down her back. "It didn't happen. You're safe now. Bogdan is no longer."

She pulled away to look into my eyes. "Is he dead?"

"Not yet, but he will be soon. Very soon."

She rested her head back on my chest. "My dad saved me. He sacrificed himself to save me," she said sadly. "Maybe, in his own way, he loves me."

"He's going to be okay," I assured her.

"He may not make it." Her voice was shaky.

This was a fact neither of us could brush aside, or deny.

"Perhaps, but he's gone through the worst part. He'll receive the best care money can buy. That should count for something."

Her hold around me tightened. 'Thank you, Levan, for being there, for getting me out of this mess. When I was hanging there on that cross, I was happy that at least I had told you I love you. Even if I had died, at least I told you the truth. And it is the truth, I love you beyond anything."

"I love you too, my darling heart. Now and forever."

EPILOGUE

BIANCA

https://www.youtube.com/watch?v=uιV8YRJnr4Q

I t was my birthday and I was feeling especially jittery.

Aldie and Biscuit came around to Levan's house earlier this morning and it had been like old times. Though we'd spoken numerous times on the phone about everything that had happened since she came back from Spain and she'd helped me get the bakery back operating again, we hadn't really got to spend quality time together. Especially with me taking care of Dad and running the bakery. Levan wanted me not to open the bakery so soon, but working actually made me feel better. I was used to working and being idle only made me worry about things I didn't need to worry over.

It felt so amazing to see her again, and I threw my arms around her. All the love I'd always felt for her flowed through me. In fact, Levan and I were preparing a surprise for her. Well, not me, I guess, more Levan. He was planning to buy her a house in a good neighborhood. It was something she would never be able to afford on her own and so I couldn't wait to see her face when we gave her the keys.

I hugged her like forever and only broke apart when Biscuit became jealous and started jumping all over the place while barking his little head off. We spent a couple of hours together and I gave her all the news of what was happening in my life.

Sarah Dale had recanted her allegations and explained that she made them up to protect her grandson. All charges against Levan had been dropped. Levan's father had come to see me one evening. He kind of gave his reluctant approval. Coming from Levan's father, it was a big compliment.

Interestingly, Levan said, Maxim might be getting married soon. To a girl from his childhood. Some kind of arranged marriage to consolidate two great families. The idea was completely foreign to me, but hey, everyone was different. I wished him nothing but a fantastic life. Without his help, Levan and I wouldn't be together today. After Aldie left, I realized I hadn't given her the most important news. I couldn't. Not until I told Levan first.

And now it was almost that time ...

My phone pinged with a text message, and I almost jumped out of my skin.

"Are you alright?" my father asked from opposite me.

I turned to him, hands covered in flour to see the concern in his gaze.

He was seated in his wheelchair, across from me in the kitchen, carefully cutting out the cookie dough I had rolled out for him.

"I'm fine." I picked up my phone and looked at it. It was only my mobile network provider telling me a price increase in line with some new government regulation. I put the phone back on the counter with a sigh.

"We need a new batch of brownies," Stacy called from the front of the bakery.

"Ready," I said and quickly went over to the sink to wash my hands. I picked up the new batch of cooled brownies and carried them over to her. When I returned to the kitchen, I was just about to continue with kneading the dough when my dad spoke.

"Levan called me last night. You both doing okay?"

I smiled, thinking of his gray eyes sparkling with such love for me, his quiet voice, full of caution, and his smile, kind and laced with mischief. "Yeah, we're doing okay."

My phone pinged again.

I pulled it out of my pocket, not caring that it was being stained with flour. I held my breath to check the message, hoping that it was from him.

It was.

I pulled it open and saw he had sent a very long message to me.

My heart began to pound in my chest as I began to read. When I realized what it was, I wanted to sink into the floor. It was the message I had sent to Levan over two years ago.

"Okay this will be long, but please read through it. I'm drowning in work right now, but I'm still going to check for your reply like every 30 seconds, even though it will pop up on my screen when it comes ... It's mentally draining, I can tell you now. How do I know? Because I'm always waiting for you to call. You see, I've fallen in love with you, Levan, and that's why I'm surprising even myself and acting like a desperate moron, telling you all this.

Maybe its karma-dang. Levan Whatever (cos I don't even know your last name. Ha, ha, how can you be in love with someone when you don't even know their last name?) But I do love you, and it's not a crush. I've had one or two of those and done abso-lutely nothing about it because it was all chemicals and it usually breaks when I trip and fall, or if I laugh too loudly).

As you probably realized I'm not one for being extrovert or wearing my heart on my sleeve, but I always wanted to be brave if I fell in love with someone.

This is me, being brave.

My initial plan was to remain close friends with you for a little while, to test if you are a maniac or something, but dude you're harder to reach, or read than a wall. Damn.

Anyway ... it's exhausting. I suspect you have no interest in this brilliant girl. But that's alright ... one man's pizza is another's salad. (Did I mention that I have an amazing sense of humor) ... And no, I'm not going to apologize for my stale jokes.

So, Levan, this might ruin whatever chance of a friendship we have and that's okay. I need to focus on work and you as a question mark in my mind is not getting me close to being the first billionaire baker (Ha, ha).

If you aren't interested, but think I'm a freaking cool girl to have as a friend, then say this outright, so I can snap back to reason real quick.

If you deem I'm not awesome enough to sit out the awkwardness then, it was great knowing you.

So ... let me know?

BIANCA

"Oh my God!" I gasped.

My shout alarmed my father. "Bianca, what's wrong?" he asked.

"Uh—nothing. I'm just about to die from shame. No wonder he never responded."

"What are you talking about?"

A new message came in then, and I read what Levan had sent.

"*We can never be friends,*" he wrote. "*I know I'm two years late but hey, you can't say I didn't give you a chance to work on becoming the first billionaire baker in the world.*"

I reread the message ... over and over again, as my eyes began to mist.

"Bianca," my dad called to me.

I swiftly wiped my eyes so as not to alarm him. "I'm fine," I assured him. "It's just Levan being sweet to me." My heart pounding in my chest, I dialed his number and put the phone to my ear.

"Hey!" I heard Levan's voice. I pulled the phone from my ear to see it was still ringing. I turned to the back door.

He stood there, his arms full of a massive bouquet of red roses.

I stared at him in shock.

"Happy birthday, my darling," he said softly.

"Uh ..." I began, just as Stacy came into the kitchen and began to giggle.

He came forward and stood in front of me. "Do you know you are covered in a ridiculous amount of flour?"

I ran my hands through my hair and more flour motes flew in front of my face.

Levan smiled and put the roses in my hand. Then he reached out and gently brushed my face with his fingers.

"Thank you," I said, suddenly shy.

"Want to go for a walk?" he asked.

I nodded. "Is it okay if I leave you here for a while?" I asked Dad.

"Ah, you go on, Love. Stacy will take care of me."

Putting the flowers down on the table, I went with Levan.

We got on the vibrant street, breezy with the late summer wind, and for a few minutes walked in complete silence.

"I wish you hadn't saved that text." Although, it was deeply touching that he had kept it all this time.

"Why?" he asked.

"It's embarrassing."

"Are you kidding me? I'm going to save that text for the rest of my life."

"Why?" I asked.

"Because it's beautiful. Every single word is beautiful. Because it's you. It's everything I want."

His hand on me burned and I remembered once again, what I had to tell him. Before I could stop myself, I rose up on my tiptoes, and pressed my lips against his.

He kissed me back as softly as I did him. Then his arms tightened almost desperately around me. Always, when we kissed it was the same. At some point, it was as if we were afraid it would be our last kiss. As if we were absolutely desperate for each other. His tongue stroked and teased mine, and I savored his flavor, in complete disbelief at how we always got to this part. No matter how many times we kissed.

When we finally broke apart, I was breathless. "I've missed you."

"I've missed you more," he replied.

I lifted my gaze to his and could see the nervousness in his eyes. "What is it?"

"I don't want to pressure you," he said. "So take your time in responding." His breathing seemed to hitch, almost as though he couldn't contain the emotion that swelled in his heart. "I have something for you." He reached into his jacket pocket.

I waited for what he would produce. For a moment, I wondered if he would produce a ring, and felt my heart nearly give out. I held my breath and watched as he instead, produced an envelope.

Surprised, but just a bit disappointed despite not wanting to admit it, I tore the envelope open to see what was inside.

It took me a while to read enough to understand, and at the realization of what it was, I gaped at him. "You bought a winery? In South Africa?"

"Yeah," he replied. "I'm gonna go off grid for a little while, do exactly what I always wanted, just like we talked about."

I let out a huge breath, my eyes misting all over again. I felt so happy, more than I could express in words. "That means you're going to leave the business?"

"Yup, as soon as I put things in order. After our wedding, we'll be on our way."

My gaze had returned to the letter but it flew upwards at what he had just said. "Uh, what?"

He dropped down to a knee right there in the middle of the sidewalk.

My hands slapped over my mouth. I thought I would faint from sheer excitement. "Levan," I breathed his name out.

He gazed up into my eyes.

The crowd that had gathered around us faded away ... in that moment, it was just me and the man I loved. He was making all of my dreams come true.

"Will you marry me, Bianca Russet?"

I was able to breathe then. I looked into his eyes and was about to respond when the cat calls urging me to accept poured in from the strangers gathering around us.

Levan laughed. "Listen to them. They know what they're talking about."

I immediately pulled him to his feet to kiss him hard and deep. "Yes," I breathed into his mouth. "Yes, Levan, I'll marry you. And yes, I'll follow you wherever you want." I glanced down at the ring then. My eyes widened even more open at the big ass, stunning baguette diamond with a halo of blue stones, presumably blue diamonds, all around it.

"Is there a problem?" he asked, the worry in his voice vibrating.

I met his gaze, not sure how to express what I was feeling. "Couldn't this buy my bakery?"

His eyes narrowed and he looked like I had rained on his parade. "It's nothing really. If you don't like it, we can get something else."

I threw my arms around him. "I love it you crazy, crazy man. What's not to love? I just wanted to know how much?"

"Ahh," he replied with amused understanding.

"More than fifty thousand?" I asked.

He looked offended.

"A hundred thousand?"

He tightened his lips to hide his smile.

My eyes widened. "Two hundred thousand?"

He put his hand out and made a small upward movement.

"Levan!" I scolded. "Three hundred?"

He made another upward movement.

The crowd behind us was going crazy.

"Nooooo," I said. "Four hundred?"

He shook his head.

"Five hundred," I stated incredulously.

"Don't go on, Bianca." He shook his head again. "It doesn't matter what it costs. The only thing you need to know is I fucking need you," he stated almost breathlessly. "Last night, I woke up in a cold sweat because I dreamed I lost you."

"You did?"

"I did and it took me hours of just lying next to you, watching you sleep before I could console myself."

"Oh, Levan," I whispered.

"The car is here," he announced excitedly and grabbed my hand.

"Levan!" I called as he pulled me along with him.

We got into the waiting SUV, and before I could say anymore, his mouth covered mine. When he lifted his head he said, "Have I got a birthday surprise for you!"

And I said, "I'm pregnant."

All the amusement fled from his face. "What?"

"My surprise is better than yours, isn't it?" I teased.

"Did you say you're *pregnant*?"

"Mm-hmm ..."

He grabbed me and held me close to him. "A little baby of our own?"

"Mm-hmm ..."

"Oh, Bianca. Bianca. Bianca. How I love you."

THE END

Hope you enjoyed Levan and Bianca's story. :) Now if you're itching to know how hard his big brother falls, get Maxim's story here:
With This Ring

COMING SOON...SAMPLE CHAPTER
SAINT & SINNER

Prologue

(10 years previously)

Willow

The fire fills two of the windows of house. Its's yellow and orange and red and it is spreading quickly, eating through the house, like a fiery revengeful monster. Soon the whole house will be up in flames. It is terrible and it is beautiful at the same time. Like a saint who turns into a sinner right before your eyes. I wish I could stay and stare at the destruction, but I can't. I have to run and pretend to call for help.

"Willow," Caleb calls over the crackling angry noises coming from the house.

I turn my head and look into his beautiful eyes. Caleb has the most beautiful eyes you ever saw. Blue, with long, thick eyelashes that should belonged to a girl. Looking into their beauty you would imagine how much he has suffered. I let myself down in those beautiful, blue starbursts for a few precious seconds. I wish we are somewhere else. I wish I'm not seeing the reflection of fire in his eyes. I wish we were born elsewhere, to different parents.

"So it's done," I whisper. I can hear the shock and wonder in my eyes. We did it. We actually did it.

He nods slowly.

"What do we do now?"

He reaches out and takes my hand in his. His hand feels hot and damp.

"We stick to the plan," he says.

"Are you afraid?" I whisper.

He shakes his head. "No. Are you?"

"I'm afraid for you," I confess.

"Don't be. I will be fine. Even if they come for me they can't do anything other than send me to a juvenile detention center. I'm tough, I can survive that, no problems. Just stick to the plan. They will try to trick you. They will try to say I have confessed, but it will all be lies. I will never admit to anything and neither should you, and no matter. This is our secret. Never tell anyone no matter how close you get to them."

"I will take this secret to my grave," I promise solemnly.

His chin juts out with determination. "So will I."

"If they don't catch you, can I contact you then."

"No," he says immediately. "It could be a trick. They should never a connection between us. After your eighteenth birthday if I am not caught we will meet at the bridge, and if I am then you can start to write to me wherever they are holding me."

I nod. All the adrenaline rushing through my blood makes me feel jittery and almost high. I clench and unclench my fingers. "Caleb, you won't forget me, will you?"

His eyes flash. "What kind of stupid question is that? Forget you? I will die for you, Willow. Are *you* planning to forget me?"

I shake my head vigorously. "Never. I love you, Caleb. More than I love myself."

His face softens. "Then let's swear it in blood."

"Alright," I agree.

He takes the knife red with the other's blood out of his belt and wipes it on the grass first. then against his pants. When it is clean he uses the sharp point of the knife to slice his finger. Blood seeps out. I hold out my hand and he moves the knife towards my flesh. As the knife touches my skin, he freezes.

I raise my head and look at him. "What is it?"

The light from the fire licks the side of his face. "I can't. I can't cut you, Willow."

"Why not?" I whisper.

"I can't hurt you."

I take the knife from his hand and prick my finger. Then we touch our bleeding fingers together. "I love you, forever," he says.

"I love you, forever," I echo.

Then he leans forward and kisses me. It is a hard, desperate kiss. The wind blows against us. And I can smell the fire in wind. Then he tears his mouth away and loops away towards the woods.

And the tears start to well up my eyes. My heart feels as if it breaking. "I will never forget you Caleb. Never," I promise into the wind. Then I start to run. I run as fast as I can, until my foot catches on something, maybe a root, and I fall backwards. My head hits something so hard, maybe a stone, it makes a cracking sound.

Pain explodes through my skull, then blackness descends.

Caleb

"You might as well admit it. I know you did it," Sheriff Winter said in an almost kind tone.

They had taken away my shoes and clothes as evidence ten hours ago and I sat in some badly fitting clothes they had given me to wear and stared at the table surface. I said nothing and planned to say nothing.

"You've been a trouble-maker all your life, and I've always turned the other way, because of your background and because I thought you were a good kid underneath it all, but now you've gone and killed a man in cold-blood, and not just any man, a man of God."

Calling that monster, a man of God was an abomination, but I didn't raise my head. I didn't speak. I didn't even ask for a lawyer. I was sticking to the script. I wouldn't react. No matter what they said.

"Why Caleb? What has he ever done to you? Why did you stab him to death and burn down his house?"

Under the table my fists clenched and slowly unclenched. No reaction. No matter the provocation. They would not trick me.

The officer suddenly slammed his palms on the table. So hard I felt the vibrations run through me. "You killed him because you wanted his niece, didn't you?

I looked up slowly and met his gaze scornfully. Was this the best he could do?

Instantly, his eyes flashed with triumph and I realized my mistake. I had reacted. Furious with myself, I looked away.

Like a terrier with a bone his changed his questioning tack. "She's a pretty girl, that Willow," he said slyly.

I said nothing. He would not trick me into responding again.

"I get why any boy would want her. If I was thirty years younger I would too. But if I was your age and I wanted a fine girl like that, I'd save up to buy her box of chocolates and take her out for an ice-cream sundae. I would kill her uncle, her only living relative. Do you know what's going to happen to her now, Caleb? They are going to come and take her away. She is going to live with strangers. Well, that is after she leaves the hospital."

I didn't even try not to react. "Hospital?" I said.

"Yes, hospital. While she was running away from the fire you started, she fell and hit her head so badly, she was out cold for many hours. And when my officers tried to question her she drew a blank about the fire and everything that has happened in the last two years. Apparently, her last memory is from a couple of days before her parents died in a car crash. She was crying and asking for her parents, and she became hysterical when she was told they died two years ago."

I stared at him in disbelief, and yet I could tell, this was no trick. He was telling the truth. Part of me was glad she wouldn't have to tell a pack of lies the other part of me felt horror that she would have to go through all that pain again. Then another thought even more horrifying than that hit me. What had happened to her memories of me? Had her mind erased me too?

"Where is she now?" I asked.

"In the hospital, sedated. They will keep under observation for a few days yet." He shrugged. "Thanks to you she has nowhere to go anyway."

I blinked. We had a plan. It was a good plan, but we didn't foresee this part.

"Look, why don't you just confess. The law will be much kinder to you if you do. You left footprints around the house. And there is a trace of blood on your pants. We'll get you."

My whole world had just fallen apart, but I looked at him

expressionlessly. In my head a little voice was saying again, and again.

"You did good, Caleb. You did good."

That same voice spoked to me as my mother, who was drunk came to see me.

"How could you," she ranted. "Everybody in town is going to hate us now."

As if to punish me, Sheriff Winter gave me no more information about Willow. "How is the girl?" I asked my mother.

She jerked her head violently with surprise that I had spoken. "She's in hospital. Why are you asking?"

I shrugged. "Would you be able to go and see her?"

Her eyes almost fell out of her face. "Are you mad? Do you know what you are saying? We are pariahs in this town now. I can't go anywhere without people spitting and snarling in my face."

"They did that before this," I reminded dryly.

She got so mad, her whole face became an ugly red. She forgot the camera and swung her hand out. Her blows were always easy to avoid, unlike my father's, and I could have if I wanted to, but I let her hit me. That would be good evidence in court.

Despite of my age, and in spite of the five people who testified about the abuse going on in my family, the jury threw the book at me. They were God-fearing folk and I had done something unforgivable. I'd a killed a representative of God.

They gave me the maximum they could give to a minor. Twenty fucking years.

"You'll be out sooner with good behavior," my court appointed solicitor said carelessly.

Not that I cared. That voice in my head had just grown stronger.

"You did good, Caleb. You did good."

Preorder here:

Saint & Sinner

ABOUT THE AUTHOR

Thank you so much for reading my book. Might you be
thinking of leaving a review? :-)
Please do it here:

With This Secret

Please click on this link to receive news of my latest releases
and great giveaways.
http://bit.ly/1oe9WdE

and remember
I **LOVE** hearing from readers so by all means come and say
hello here:

ALSO BY GEORGIA LE CARRE

Owned

42 Days

Besotted

Seduce Me

Love's Sacrifice

Masquerade

Pretty Wicked (novella)

Disfigured Love

Hypnotized

Crystal Jake 1,2&3

Sexy Beast

Wounded Beast

Beautiful Beast

Dirty Aristocrat

You Don't Own Me 1 & 2

You Don't Know Me

Blind Reader Wanted

Redemption

The Heir

Blackmailed By The Beast

Submitting To The Billionaire

The Bad Boy Wants Me

Printed in Great Britain
by Amazon

25803121R00189